Jordan's Stormy Banks

JEFFERSON BASS

JORDAN'S STORMY BANKS

A BODY FARM NOVELLA

WM
WILLIAM MORROW
An Imprint of HarperCollinsPublishers

Excerpt from *Cut to the Bone* copyright © 2013 by Jefferson Bass LLC.

EPub Edition SEPTEMBER 2013 ISBN: 9780062320308
Print Edition ISBN: 9780062320315

10 9 8

On Jordan's stormy banks I stand,
and cast a wishful eye
to Canaan's fair and happy land,
where my possessions lie.

I am bound for the promised land,
I am bound for the promised land;
oh, who will come and go with me?
I am bound for the promised land.

SAMUEL STENNETT

To all the brave men and women who have
stood, and have marched, and have strived—
and who still strive—for justice and equality.

"Civilization . . . has spread a veneer over the surface of the soft-shelled animal known as man. It is a very thin veneer; but so wonderfully is man constituted that he squirms on his bit of achievement and believes he is garbed in armor-plate. Yet man today is the same man that drank from his enemy's skull in the dark German forests, that sacked cities, and stole his women from neighboring clans like any howling aborigine . . . Starve him, let him miss six meals, and see gape through the veneer the hungry maw of the animal beneath. Get between him and the female of his kind upon whom his mating instinct is bent, and see his eyes blaze like an angry cat's, hear in his throat the scream of wild stallions, and watch his fists clench like an orangutan's . . . It requires a slightly different stick to scrape [the veneer] off. The raw animals beneath are identical."

JACK LONDON, "The Somnambulists," 1906

Perimortem, Part I

perimortem *(adjective): at or around the time of death*

December 24, 1990

THE FLAMES FLARED WITHIN the darkness, swirling red and orange and oily black, as the cross caught fire on the courthouse lawn. Lit and shadowed by the fiery undulations, as if in a nightmare, I saw angry faces, oiled guns, and the tight, heavy coils of a noose.

But it was no nightmare. I was wide-awake, it was Christmas Eve, and it was not entirely clear to me who would be found swaying from the noose by the light of Christmas morning: the black man huddled inside the Morgan County jail, or the meddlesome scientist standing on the building's steps, his back—*my* back—pressed tight against the wooden door.

How had it come to this? Was I wrong about the century I inhabited? Had I somehow been transported back in time a hundred years, from 1990 to 1890? How had matters come to this—for the man behind bars, and especially for me? Had I spoken out of turn, or rushed in where angels fear to tread? Maybe I should have stayed in Kansas instead of taking the job in Tennessee.

Or maybe it was all just because of the memo. That damned memo . . .

1

Antemortem

antemortem *(adjective): occurring before the time of death*

July 4, 1990

I STARED AT THE stinky, sodden mess on the stainless-steel gurney, my eyes watering and my brain reeling. "What am I supposed to do with this?" I asked the man who'd just delivered the mess, which was a corpse he'd pulled from the back of a hearse and wheeled into the basement of Neyland Stadium. Above our heads reared the stadium itself, the University of Tennessee's massive shrine to college football. Around us—in the dingy basement room I'd grandly named the Osteology Laboratory—clustered a few government-surplus lab tables and a few thousand boxes of Indian bones, so recently arrived and unloaded that they'd not even been shelved yet.

The hearse driver, who worked for a funeral home in Crossville, seventy miles west of Knoxville, shrugged. He pulled a piece of paper from his shirt pocket, unfolded it, and glanced at the wording. "I guess you're supposed to do whatever the Chief M.E. says you'll do," he said. He handed the page to me. "Welcome to Tennessee," he said, then spun on his heel and scuttled away in the hearse before I could stop him.

I read the memo with a mixture of puzzlement and rising alarm.

Date: July 1, 1990
To: Tennessee Medical Examiners
From: Dr. Gerald Francis, M.D.,
  Chief Medical Examiner
Subject: Dr. Bill Brockton, State
  Forensic Anthropologist

I am pleased to announce that I have appointed Dr. Bill Brockton to the newly created position of Tennessee State Forensic Anthropologist, effective immediately.

Dr. Brockton has just been hired as chairman of the Anthropology Department at the University of Tennessee in Knoxville. He comes to UT after ten years on the faculty at the University of Kansas in Lawrence, as well as ten summers of field work in South Dakota, where he and his students excavated thousands of eighteenth and nineteenth century Arikara Indian skeletons. Dr. Brockton received his

Ph.D. at the University of Pennsylvania; his mentor, Dr. Wilton Krogman, was one of the nation's foremost physical anthropologists, sometimes called "the Sherlock Holmes of bones."

As State Forensic Anthropologist, Dr. Brockton is available to examine any unidentified remains found in your county, as well as identified corpses that have, or might have, skeletal trauma. I am confident that Dr. Brockton will be a strong and valuable addition to our staff, and I trust that you will all extend him a warm Tennessee welcome.

Cc: Tennessee District Attorneys General
Tennessee Sheriffs
Dr. Bill Brockton, Ph.D.

I reread the memo. Three times. "Crap, Gerry," I muttered, as if Gerry—Chief Medical Examiner Gerald Francis—could hear me, despite the fact that he was 180 miles away, in Nashville. "Why didn't you run that past me before you sent it out all over the damn state?" Thanks to the memo, every M.E. and D.A. and sheriff, in however-the-hell-many counties my new home state had, had gotten the wrong idea about me.

The appointment itself was no surprise—I'd agreed to take the post—and it wasn't the memo's description of my education and experience that had me fretting. When it came to analyzing skeletal remains and skeletal trauma, I felt competent and even confident; I had, after all, studied some ten thousand skeletons over the past dozen years, half of them in the dusty collections of the Smithsonian Institution, half of them in the fine-grained soil of the Great Plains, where I'd found and excavated them just ahead of rising waters, on rivers newly dammed by the U.S. Army Corps of Engineers. "The legions of the dammed," one of my waggish students had dubbed the five thousand or so Indian skeletons I'd saved from watery graves.

No, what troubled me about the memo was its promise of what I could do—what I *would* do—for the state's far-flung M.E.'s: "examine any unidentified remains," as well as "identified corpses that have, or might have, skeletal trauma."

I'd consulted with law enforcement investigators for years in Kansas, before moving to Tennessee; that consulting work, in fact, was how Gerry Francis knew me— from a case I'd described at a forensic conference a few years before. My collaborations with law enforcement had begun by accident, or, more accurately, by happenstance: One summer early in my teaching career at Kansas, as my students and I were pulling Indian bones from the shoreline, a South Dakota sheriff's deputy had jounced to a stop at the dig site and asked if I'd be willing to examine a skeleton a rancher had found in a dry wash on his property and tell him whatever I could about it. "A skeleton's a skeleton," I'd told the deputy. "Sure, let's go."

The skeleton—a robust white male—bore a striking resemblance to many of the male Indian skeletons I'd dug from their compact, circular graves: the skull struck by a heavy blunt object, which had left an oval depression—

remarkably similar to that created by a Sioux war club. As it turned out, the dead white man actually *had* been struck by a Sioux war club. The man was a relic poacher, and—in a case of ironic just desserts—he'd been killed by a rival collector in a struggle over the club: a trophy that had emerged from a century of retirement to become once more a lethal weapon.

After I helped the sheriff's office with that case, one thing had led to another, as things have a way of doing, and by the time I'd left Kansas for Tennessee, I was averaging six or eight forensic cases a year for local police, county sheriffs, and the Kansas Bureau of Investigation.

But those six or eight cases invariably involved dry, weathered bones, not slimy, stinking corpses like the one that had just been delivered to me. *Dumped on me, more like it*, I thought. I could picture the relief—the utter delight—the Cumberland County medical examiner must have felt when he read his boss's memo and realized that he could wash his hands of this body, literally and figuratively, by sending it to Knoxville. To me.

As I unzipped the body bag and folded back the large, C-shaped flap that formed the bag's upper surface, I jumped back, startled and repulsed by the sudden sight and sound of thousands of maggots—blowfly larva—swarming and squirming and writhing to escape the light to which I'd suddenly exposed them. Diving for cover, they quickly slithered into the large openings they'd created in the face, neck, and lower abdomen of the body; as I watched their swift migration, my revulsion gave way to scientific fascination. Once they were out of sight, though, my gaze strayed back to the memo. *God, how many more bodies like this am I gonna get?* I wondered silently. Aloud, looking back at the body once more, I repeated, "What am I supposed to do with this?"

I was still without an answer an hour later when the phone rang. I started to ignore it—it was July Fourth, after all—but remembered that I'd given Kathleen, my wife, the bone lab's number. "I'll only be a minute," I'd told her. "Just long enough to sign for some skeletal remains. Call me if you need me to pick up anything on the way home."

"Hello?"

"Bill?" She sounded surprised to hear my voice, and that in turn surprised me, since I'd given her the number and told her that this was where I'd be.

"Hi, honey," I said. "What's up? Need something?"

"I need *you.* We have fifty people showing up for this cookout in twenty minutes. Your new colleagues and my new colleagues and our new neighbors. You said you'd be home half an hour ago to help."

I checked my watch and felt myself wince. "Oh, crap—I'm sorry. This turned out to be more complicated than I expected. I'm leaving right now."

As I hung up the phone, my earlier, unresolved question continued to hang in the air, nearly as tangible as the odor from the body on the gurney. Then inspiration came to me. "Ah," I said to the corpse. "*That's* what I'll do with you."

2

IT HAD SEEMED LIKE a good idea at the time, but in hindsight, perhaps what I'd done with the corpse hadn't been so inspired after all.

The building that was shoehorned beneath the grandstands of Neyland Stadium—a wedge-shaped warren of grimy rooms named Stadium Hall—had begun its life, decades before, as an athletic dormitory. Now, deemed too dilapidated to house athletes, it housed the Anthropology Department. Stadium Hall's chief virtues, as best I could tell during my first week on the job, were two: It contained plenty of rooms—hundreds of rooms—to accommodate what I hoped would be a fast-growing population of Anthropology faculty and graduate students. It also contained an abundance of bathrooms and showers, and it was in one of these showers—the one in the stairwell adjoining the basement bone lab—that I'd decided to stash the corpse over the July Fourth holiday, until I could figure out how best to clean and examine the bones of the dead man.

I returned to the stadium to reclaim the remains at 9:00 A.M. on July fifth. Unfortunately, the building's janitor had returned at 8:00 A.M., and by the time I showed up, he was mad as a hornet. The university police officers summoned by the janitor were none too happy, either.

I explained the situation to the police officers briefly, showing them the memo about my appointment as State Forensic Anthropologist, and then phoned the Cumberland County medical examiner, so he could corroborate my story—something he did with evident amusement. *Great,* I thought as the grinning police officers departed. *I'll never hear the end of this—not from the campus police, and not from the M.E.'s, either.*

It had taken only twenty minutes to resolve the police officers' concerns. Not so those of the janitor, who, rightly or wrongly, considered Stadium Hall his territory, not mine, and who threatened me with a smorgasbord of dire fates if he ever found another rotting corpse in his building. "I don't mind all them Indian bones you got in them boxes," he said. "But this-here nastiness ain't got no place in my building. I want it out of here, and I don't mean tomorrow."

"It'll be gone by the end of the day," I assured him, wondering how on earth I would manage to keep that promise.

"You've got a *what* in one of the showers in Stadium Hall?" The dean of the College of Arts and Sciences—my new boss, as of four days before—sounded groggy when he answered the phone, and the thought that I'd awakened him during a five-day holiday weekend made me wince.

"A decomposing body," I repeated. I explained the situation to him. It was the third time in an hour I'd summarized the series of unexpected events, hasty decisions, and unhappy consequences.

"And what, exactly, do you want me to do about this?" He no longer sounded groggy; he sounded wide-awake and more than a little annoyed.

"Here's the thing," I said. "I think I need some land to put bodies on. The Cumberland County medical examiner isn't the only one likely to send me rotting John Does. The way this memo reads, bodies will be coming in from all over the state. It wasn't a problem out in Kansas— Kansas is twice the size of Tennessee, with only half as many people. So out there, it takes a while for folks to be found, and by that time they're generally down to nice, dry bone. Here, on the other hand . . ."

He sighed. "I'll make some calls." I felt my spirits lift, but they plummeted a moment later when he added, "First thing Monday."

"Monday? But that's four days from now," I squawked. "What am I supposed to do with this guy for the next four days?"

"You're a bright young man," he said. "You'll think of something."

"You've got a *what* in the back of your truck?" Kathleen stared at me as if I'd lost my mind.

"A decomposing body." I explained the situation yet again; by now I could have told the story in my sleep.

"Where—*here*? In *our garage*?"

"No, no. Of course not. I'm not *that* dumb."

"How dumb are you? Did you leave it parked somewhere at UT?"

"Uh, not exactly," I hedged. She gave me a gimlet-eyed look, waiting me out. "It's in the driveway. Halfway between the house and the street."

"Bill *Brockton*," she groaned. "What am I supposed to do with you?"

"Hey, it could be worse," I pointed out.

"How, exactly?"

"I could've brought him home *before* the cookout."

She shook her head and heaved a sigh. "Thank heaven for small favors," she muttered.

The dean summoned me to his office at mid-morning Monday. By that time the cab of my truck smelled to high heaven, even though the body bag was back in the cargo bed. I'd driven to campus with the windows down and my head in the wind, like a dog's.

As I left the stadium for the walk up the hill to the dean's office, I noticed a thick cloud of flies surrounding the truck; on the camper shell's window screens, they were packed wing-to-wing, as tightly as planes on an air-craft carrier's deck.

An hour later, trailing a plume of flies in my wake, I pulled away from the stadium and threaded my way up the Tennessee River, a map open on the seat beside me. Six miles to the east—where the French Broad and the Holston rivers converged to form the Tennessee—the university owned a farm where, for half a century, the College of Agriculture had raised pigs. The pig-farming venture had ended a few years before, and the old sow barn, where countless piglets had been born and nursed, now sat empty and idle. That barn, the dean had informed me in our brief, curt meeting, was the place—the *only* place—where I was to warehouse any corpses I happened to receive from my colleagues in the medical examiner's system.

"Empty and idle" were accurate descriptors, as far as they went, but they were not comprehensive. A complete description of the sow barn—*my* sow barn—required "crumbling and stinking," too. *Fair enough*, I realized, considering that I'd be contributing more than a little decay and odor to the property myself.

I backed the truck up to the barn, opened the cargo shell and tailgate, then slid the body bag out. It dropped to the ground with a dull, squishy thud. By the time I dragged it across the wooden threshold and into the dim, foul-smelling interior of the barn, the bag and I were already being buzzed by a new squadron of flies.

"Welcome to Tennessee," I said to myself.

3

December 21, 1990

TURNING BACK FROM THE office doorway, I snatched up the ringing phone. "Hi, honey," I said. "I'll be right there. I'm leaving this instant." It was the Friday before Christmas, and all through the stadium I was the only creature stirring; everyone else was already home for the holidays, or at least en route.

I was answered by a gravelly, homespun voice, half an octave deeper than my own. "Well, darlin', I sure 'preciate that," the man chuckled. "But before you go, you reckon you could connect me with a Dr. Brockman? Dr. Bill Brockman?"

I felt my face redden. "Sorry," I said. "I thought you were my wife. This is Dr. Brockton. How can I help you?"

"This is Sheriff Dixon, Dr. Brockman. Up in Morgan County."

"Hello, Sheriff," I said. "It's Brock-*ton*, by the way,

not Brockman. What can I do for you?" Turning to the framed Tennessee map mounted on the wall, I scanned for Morgan County. The state had ninety-five counties, and in the six months since my arrival in Knoxville, I'd worked ten forensic cases—five of them in Knox County; one each in Chattanooga, Nashville, and Memphis; the janitor-infuriating case from Cumberland County, fifty miles to the west; and one from a rural county southeast of Knoxville. I seemed to recall that Morgan County was nearby, but I was having trouble finding it.

"Looks like maybe we've got a homicide up here. A hiker found a body in the woods, up in Frozen Head State Park. Unidentified nigrah woman. In pretty rough shape. The medical examiner took one look and told me to call and have you come get her. Reckon you could come on up this way?"

I felt a tinge of annoyance—*that damned memo*, I thought again—followed by a wave of excitement and then a ripple of guilt. My addiction to forensic adrenaline was, I suspected, as strong as any alcoholic's thirst, and the truth was, I was happy to have a chance to slake it. But I'd promised Kathleen I'd be home by five o'clock, to help prepare for a Christmas party at six. "Where's the body now, Sheriff?"

"Still in the woods. Just up the slope from a creek. Jordan Branch. It's about five miles outside Wartburg. The M.E. said to leave it at the scene for you."

I spotted Wartburg on the map—a small dot about fifty miles northwest of Knoxville—and then found the irregular green rectangle that marked the state park. Glancing

out the office windows, through the grime on the glass
and the latticework of girders supporting the stadium's
grandstands, I saw that the sky had already gone dark. "I
don't mean to put you off, Sheriff," I said, "but I'd rather
work the scene in the daylight. No matter how good your
lights are, it's easy to miss things in the dark. Any chance
you could post somebody out there tonight, to keep an
eye on things? Let me meet you there first thing in the
morning?"

He considered this for a moment. "I reckon I could
put Cotterell out there. One of my deputies. He ain't got
nothin' better to do."

I got directions and agreed to meet him at the Morgan
County courthouse the next morning at nine. After hanging up, I called Kathleen. "Hi, honey," I said with a sense
of déjà vu, sheepishness, and amusement. "I'll be right
there. I'm leaving this instant."

4

"PRETTY ROUGH SHAPE" WAS putting it mildly. *Very* mildly. The truth was, in ten years of forensic casework, I'd never seen such a shocking death scene as the one Sheriff Dixon led me to.

We'd met at the Morgan County courthouse, a quaint brick building topped by an elegant, four-sided white cupola, each side dominated by a large clock face reading 9:05.

Ten minutes later, after backtracking several miles along the Knoxville highway, we'd turned onto a small side road that led to two destinations, according to a green sign at the turnoff: Frozen Head State Park, and Morgan County Correctional Center. The prison was first, a sprawling complex of dull brown brick and gleaming razor wire. A mile or so later, after a sharp turn and a narrow bridge over a tumbling creek—Jordan Branch, I guessed—we'd entered a narrow wooded valley. FROZEN HEAD STATE PARK, read a sign, its white-painted letters etched into dark brown boards. Two miles beyond the sign—past a gate marked AUTHORIZED VEHICLES ONLY, where asphalt gave way to gravel—we'd stopped behind a Morgan County Sheriff's Office cruiser and a black Ford Crown Victoria sporting a state government tag, a trunk-mounted radio antenna, and a side spotlight near the left outside mirror.

The body lay barely thirty yards from the road, within a ragged rectangle of crime-scene tape strung from tree trunks. The ground sloped down toward the creek, and as we picked our way through the rocky terrain, I saw that the legs were angled downhill, toward the stream.

The corpse—a woman's corpse—was nude, and when we got close enough to make out details, I felt my stomach lurch. The body was bloated, the abdomen swollen with gases produced by bacteria and enzymes in the digestive tract. The skin of the torso, arms, and legs was largely intact, but virtually no soft tissue remained on the neck and face; the jaws and teeth were bared in a macabre grin, and the cheekbones and eye orbits—now vacant—were exposed as well, along with the vertebrae of the neck. So were the lower ends of the legs, the tibia and fibula of each leg jutting, footless, from the shredded flesh of the shins.

But gruesome as all those features were, they weren't what I found shocking about the scene. What I found shocking was the way the woman's body had been posed. Her legs were splayed on either side of a small tree, and her crotch—her decaying, decomposing crotch—was pressed tight against the trunk, as if, even long after death, she were still being sexually violated.

"Hey. *Doc*." The sheriff's gravelly voice tugged at the sleeve of my consciousness, and the insistent tone made me suspect that he'd called my name more than once.

"Sorry, what?" I looked in the direction his voice had come from, and saw him standing by two other men— one in uniform, the other in civilian clothes.

"This here's my deputy, Jim Cotterell. And this troublemaker"—he said it in a tone that might have been joking, or might not—"is Bubba Hardknot, our friendly neighborhood agent from the Tennessee Bureau of Investigation."

"Deputy," I said, shaking the hand of the man in uniform. Then I extended my hand to the TBI agent. "Sorry, I didn't quite catch your name?"

"Special Agent Meffert," he said, smiling slantwise, in a way I couldn't quite interpret. "Wellington Meffert. It's a little fancy for everyday use in Morgan County. Most folks around here call me Bubba Hardknot. When they're being polite."

"I'm kindly surprised to see you way up here in the woods on a Saturday morning, Bubba," said the sheriff flatly. "I thought you TBI types kept banker's hours. Cotterell call you?" He glanced at his deputy; the look seemed accusatory or even hostile, and I gathered there was no love lost between the sheriff and the TBI agent— and possibly not between the sheriff and his own deputy.

"Naw, the park rangers called me," Meffert replied casually. "State property, state agency. Go figure."

"Hmm," grunted Dixon.

My camera was slung around my neck, and I removed the lens cap and began taking pictures—wide shots of the entire scene first, then increasingly tight ones, spiraling in so that I photographed the body from all angles. I finished the 36-exposure roll with close-ups of the footless legs, the fleshless neck and face, and the obscenely posed crotch. Satisfied that I'd captured the key images, I stood from my crouch and turned to the law enforcement officers. "Any idea who she is?"

The sheriff answered. "Not yet. Shouldn't take too long to find out, though. We don't get too many dead nigrahs around here." He chuckled, then added, "Not near enough, right fellas?" He gave me a sly grin and a wink. I blinked, puzzled—and disbelieving, once I replayed his words and decided that I'd understood the joke correctly. I glanced at the other men's faces. Deputy Cotterell was looking away, his cheeks flaming; Agent Meffert's face was a blank mask, as expressionless as stone.

I cleared my throat and turned back toward the body. "She might not actually be negroid," I said. "Once a person's been dead a few days, you can't always tell the race from the color of the skin. The skin of Caucasoids—whites—often darkens as they decay." The sheriff frowned, perhaps because he doubted what I'd said, perhaps because he didn't like the idea that the dead woman might be white. I couldn't tell which was the case, and I didn't want to know. "Any women been reported missing?"

The sheriff shook his head. "Naw. No nigrahs I've heard tell of. For sure no white women."

Reaching into my back pocket, I pulled out a pair of latex gloves and tugged them on, then knelt beside the head for a closer look at the exposed bones of the face. The woman's teeth had a strongly vertical orientation, and the nasal opening was narrow, with a thin sill of bone jutting slightly from the base of the opening. "Now that I look closer," I said, "I'm pretty sure she's white."

"The hell you say," muttered the sheriff.

"What makes you think that, Doc?" asked Meffert quickly.

I glanced over my shoulder. "You got a pen on you, Agent Meffert?" He nodded. I held a gloved index finger to my lips, as if I were a librarian, mid-shush. "Put one end of the pen at the base of your nose and lay it across your lips." Looking intrigued, he did as I'd directed. "It touches your chin, right?" He nodded again, the pen still in place. "If you were black, it wouldn't."

"Wouldn't what?" interrupted the sheriff.

"Wouldn't touch the chin. Black people's teeth and jaws slope forward—the fancy, five-dollar term for that is 'prognathic.' White people's teeth and jaws are more vertical—'orthognic.' This woman's got a narrow nasal opening, too; blacks have a wide one, with vertical grooves—gutters—so they can take in more air through their nose. That's evolution at work, adapting them to tropical climates."

Meffert nodded, looking thoughtful. The sheriff scowled, looking . . . *scowly*. He opened his mouth to speak, and I half expected to hear the term "jungle bunnies" in response to my evolutionary explanation. Instead, he asked, "You a bettin' man, Doc?"

"Excuse me?"

"You a bettin' man? A gambler?"

"Not really," I said.

"Well, if you was, what kind of odds would you lay on this being a white woman?"

"How certain I am that she's white, based on the teeth and jaws and nasal opening?"

"Right."

I shrugged. "I hate to say a hundred percent, because if I turn out to be wrong, I'll look like a hundred-percent idiot. I'll be able to look at a couple other things once I get her back to the lab and clean off the bones. But right here, right now? Ninety-five percent." I tugged downward on the mandible, opening the jaws so I could inspect the lower teeth, especially the molars. "Middle or upper income, too, probably. She's had good dental care."

The sheriff rubbed the corners of his mouth with one hand, his thumb and fingers widening and narrowing repeatedly, his lips alternately stretching and pursing in artificial simulacra of smiles and frowns. Then he turned slightly to one side and spat, a long stream of tobacco juice and saliva arcing onto the ground a foot from where I knelt. "Son of a bitch," he said. "He done this to a *white* woman? They's some serious shit about to hit the fan here. Ain't no doubt about it. We got to catch that boy, y'all hear me?"

"You think this murder was committed by a *juvenile*?"

By the time I finished asking the question, I realized how foolish it was.

"A man—a black man—escaped from Brushy four days ago," said Meffert. "He's still on the loose."

"Brushy?"

"Brushy Mountain State Prison."

"The one we passed on the way in?"

"No. The old prison, in Petros." He pointed across the creek, as if I might be able to see it if I looked. "It's close— three, four five miles, as the crow flies—but there's one hell of a mountain between here and there."

The prison's name rang a bell in the back of my mind. "Seems like I remember that somebody famous did time in Brushy Mountain."

Meffert nodded. "Still *doing* time. James Earl Ray. Guy that assassinated Martin Luther King. Sentenced to ninety-nine years."

"It's a hunnerd, now," interjected the deputy, Cotterell. "Remember? They tacked on one more year after he escaped."

"Oh yeah," I said. "What about that? I thought that prison was famous for being escape-proof."

"Ain't no prison escape-proof," scoffed the sheriff. "Not if it's built by human hands, guarded by human guards. Ray and six others scaled a fence in the back corner of the yard one day. Maybe the guards was sleepin' on the job. Maybe they was *paid* to be sleepin' on the job. Dumbasses went the wrong damn way after they got out, though."

"They headed north," Meffert explained. "This way. Into the mountains. They were caught two days later, in some of the toughest terrain in Tennessee. Story goes, by the time they found him, Ray was so exhausted and hungry and tore up, he was *begging* to go back to Brushy."

"And this guy who escaped four days ago," I said. "What's his story? Also a killer?"

"If he weren't before, he for damn sure is *now*," said the sheriff. "He is a sack of human excrement." The other two nodded.

"Serial sex offender," said the TBI agent.

"Bad luck for this poor gal, crossing paths with him," the sheriff resumed. "She didn't never have no chance."

As the lawmen continued chatting and head-shaking, I unfolded a body bag and laid it beside the woman's remains. The task of getting her into the bag was complicated by the presence of the sapling between her legs. I considered lifting one of her legs to vertical and then swinging it clear of the tree—the corpse had already passed through rigor mortis—but I feared that bending the leg so far might tear it from the hip. Instead, I squatted above the head and worked my hands under the shoulders, into the armpits, and slid the corpse several feet up the hill, so that both legs were clear of the tree. Then I repositioned the bag, unzipped it, and folded back the top. "Could one of you guys give me a hand?"

They looked at one another, no one moving. Finally Sheriff Dixon said, "Jim, get over there and help the perfessor." Cotterell grimaced but complied.

"There's another pair of gloves sticking out of my back pocket," I said. "You're gonna want those, I'm thinking." He tugged them free and pulled them on. "Let's lift her legs and swing those over first," I said, "then her upper body." He nodded and took hold of the left shin, while I grasped the right, wishing the feet were still there to help keep my grip from slipping loose. "Okay, on three, we lift and swing. One, two, *three*."

With a lift, accompanied by a grunt from the stocky deputy, we got her legs and pelvis onto the rubberized fabric.

"Okay, same thing with the arms." He nodded, and we hoisted and swung the upper body onto the bag, then I folded the flap across the body and tugged the C-shaped zipper closed. Then, with the added help of the sheriff and the TBI agent, we lugged the bag up the slope and slid it into the back of my truck.

I took my leave of the sheriff, his deputy, and Special Agent Bubba, promising to fax a preliminary report by Tuesday. Meffert raised his eyebrows. "You know that's Christmas Day, right?"

"Crap," I said. "No, I forgot. How about Wednesday, the twenty-sixth?"

Meffert shrugged; the sheriff nodded, allowing as how he reckoned that would be all right. I removed the gloves and tossed them in the back of the truck, and motioned for Cotterell to do likewise, then closed the tailgate and the shell.

I drove slowly down the park's narrow road and rumbled across Jordan Branch, then sped up as the road straightened and widened near the prison. Ten minutes after I turned onto the highway toward Knoxville, I noticed another two-lane road, state route 116, T-ing in from the left. PETROS 2 said a sign pointing up 116. BRUSHY MOUNTAIN STATE PRISON 3. On a whim, I slowed and took the turn.

Petros was a cluster of modest homes—a few dozen or so—plus a handful of small churches, several dilapidated repair shops, a cinder-block grocery store, and a volunteer fire department. A mile beyond what passed for downtown—just before the highway made a hairpin turn and started angling up a mountainside—I came to the turnoff for Brushy Mountain.

The prison occupied the back end of a small, deep valley—a hollow, or "holler," in East Tennessee dialect—and even from a quarter mile away, the façade was forbidding: a huge, brooding fortress of stone, topped by castlelike crenellations and flanked on three sides by steep forested mountains, as if the prison itself had taken up a defensive position and were making its last stand. And in a way, perhaps it was, for Agent Meffert had said that the state was planning to close the facility, as soon as the Morgan County Correctional Complex could be expanded to accommodate Brushy's hard-core convicts.

Idling toward the grim stone fortress, I imagined James Earl Ray and six other desperate men scaling the fence, then scrambling up the steep, rocky slopes toward Frozen Head. Was that the same route this latest fugitive had taken—the sack-of-excrement "boy" Sheriff Dixon was intent on capturing? Had he gotten farther than Ray? And had his path crossed with that of an unlucky hiker—a woman who happened to be in a terribly wrong place at a fatally wrong time?

As I crept forward, I noticed a patrol car leave the prison's gate and head in my direction. Then—imagining the scene that might ensue if I were stopped and the back of my truck searched—I made a hasty U-turn and headed back toward the highway, and the comforts of UT.

By most measures, Stadium Hall was a shithole. But compared to Brushy Mountain, it was the lap of luxury. A lavish, lustrous ivory tower.

5

"NO WAY. I CAN'T bring that inside," said Dr. Kimbrough, wrinkling his nose as he peered down at the body bag. My truck was backed up to the loading dock at UT Medical Center, and I'd slid the body bag onto the dock and unzipped it just enough to show the skull to Kimbrough, the young radiology resident unlucky enough to be spending Saturday evening on call. "No way," he repeated. "The attending would have my head on a platter."

"He won't even know," I pleaded. "It's the weekend, the E.R.'s quiet right now—the drunk-driving accidents and bar fights don't rev up till midnight—and I really, really need to know if there's a bullet somewhere in her."

"Won't even *know*? Are you kidding?" He gave a barkish laugh. "We'd have patients and hospital staff running for the exits, puking as they ran." I had to admit, he might have a point there. "Isn't there some other way to tell if there's a bullet in her?"

There was a way, actually—sift through all the liquid and goo I'd get when I simmered the soft tissue off the bones—but I didn't want to wait that long or work that hard, so I hedged. "Look, this is life-and-death stuff. Somebody's killed this woman, and I'm desperately trying to figure out who, and how. I've got a county sheriff and a TBI agent breathing down my neck so hard my wife's starting to get jealous."

He smiled, but the smile was followed by a head shake. "We cannot take that inside. Not negotiable. What I *can* do, though, is bring the portable X-ray machine down here and shoot some films here on the dock. We don't even have to take her out of the bag."

"How's the quality?"

"Not great. Best you're gonna get, though—from me at least—so take it or leave it." He saw the doubt on my face. "Look, if there's a lump of lead in there, it'll light up that film like a full moon at midnight."

It was a dark and moonless night, figuratively and forensically speaking: The woman's corpse did not contain a bright round bullet, I saw when I reviewed the films with Kimbrough. That didn't surprise me, as I'd noticed no entry or exit wound in the intact regions of the body.

What *did* surprise me—what stunned me, in fact, when I saw the X ray of the head—was the brilliant latticework of metal in the woman's skull: four flat, L-shaped brackets of metal, screwed to the upper jaw. At some point the woman's face had been bolted back together. "Holy crap,"

I said to the radiologist. "She must've taken one hell of a blow to the teeth."

He nodded. "That's a classic LeFort fracture," he said. "Car wreck? She take a steering wheel in the face?"

"I have no idea. All I know is, that's not what killed her."

"Type One," he went on, as if we were making medical rounds. "Horizontal fracture plane in the maxilla, just below the nose, detaching the teeth and palate. Could've been worse," he added, his index finger tracing an arc above the woman's nose. "A LeFort Type Two breaks off the entire maxilla and the nasal bone—wiggle the teeth, and the whole nose wiggles. A Type Three breaks off the zygomatic bones, too, so the whole face hangs down. This lady was lucky."

"Tell her, not me," I said. "Oh, you can't—she's dead." He flushed, and I felt bad for him. But not as bad as I felt for her. "Sorry. Thanks for the help—I do appreciate it." I tugged the bag off the loading dock and into the truck, then headed back toward the stadium. Crossing the river, I glanced upstream at the black, cold waters of the Tennessee spooling past Knoxville and the university, wondering what dark currents had swept this woman to her fate. I still didn't know who she was or how she'd died, but I now felt confident of identifying her. Whoever had done the dental and facial surgery would surely remember it. All I had to do was find that person.

I parked a hundred yards from Stadium Hall, the truck backed up to a corrugated metal building labeled ANTHROPOLOGY ANNEX. The Annex, like the sow barn, had been conferred on me by the dean in the wake of what was now widely known as "the Shower Incident," when the janitor had found the rotting corpse I'd stashed overnight. On a scale of one to ten, the Annex rated a minus three; the uninsulated metal structure was an oven in summer and in icebox in winter. Still, it had plumbing and electricity. More to the point, it had no other tenants . . . and it had a steam-jacketed kettle, an immense cauldron that—over the course of twenty-four simmering hours—could transform a decomposing body into a clean skeleton.

I opened the back of the truck, then wheeled a gurney from the Annex and slid the body bag onto it. I rolled it across the concrete floor and into the processing room, which contained a long counter, a bathtub-sized sink, and the steam-jacketed kettle. Opening a tap, I began filling the kettle with hot water; as it filled, I dumped in a half cup of Adolph's Meat Tenderizer and a cup of Biz laundry powder—my secret ingredients, to help soften the tissue and sweeten the smell. Once the kettle was full and the tap was off, I noticed a faint noise coming from direction of the body bag. *Crap*, I thought, warily unzipping the bag to reveal teeming masses of maggots, which had emerged from the torso's interior during the long, dark ride back from Morgan County. In the quiet of the Annex, I could hear them, and the sound of their moist wriggling and chewing bore a striking, unsettling similarity to the *snap crackle pop* of Rice Krispies—a breakfast I vowed, then and there, never to eat again.

I glanced up at the clock on the wall: 6:43 P.M. *Crap*, I

thought again, *I'm late for supper, and where the hell is Bohanan?* Art Bohanan was a forensic specialist with the Knoxville Police Department, and his area of particular expertise was fingerprints. I'd worked on a case with Art several months before, and I'd watched, astonished, as he took a shriveled husk of skin that had sloughed off from a dead man's hand, moistened it, and then lifted a perfect set of prints. The Morgan County sheriff had scoffed at my suggestion that we try to get prints from the Jordan Branch corpse, and even the TBI agent, Meffert, had shaken his head dismissively. But I wasn't willing to give up without trying, so on the way back to Knoxville I'd stopped at a gas station and phoned Art to ask for help. He'd agreed to meet me at six-thirty. So why wasn't he here?

Just as I was headed for the phone to send a nagging page, the building's corrugated wall boomed like thunder, and then the door screeched open. "Shoo-*eee*," came Art's folksy drawl. "Either there's a really ripe one in here, or you are wearing the world's nastiest aftershave."

I grinned. "I don't particularly care for it, but it's my wife's favorite, and I do try to please her."

"She's one lucky woman."

"Thanks for coming. You're my only hope for fingerprints. Even the TBI agent threw up his hands."

"But why was a TBI agent eatin' his hands in the first place?"

"Man," I groaned, "and people say *my* puns are bad." I folded back the flap of the body bag to expose both arms, then lifted the left one by the wrist, palm up. "What do you think—can you get usable prints?"

"I believe so," he said, leaning down to study the fingers. "Can you give me a hand?"

"Sure. How can I help?"

"Give. Me. A hand." I stared at him, puzzled; he stared back with an expression of weary patience on his face, as if waiting for a slow-witted child to grasp the simplest of instructions. Finally he rolled his eyes and, with the blade of his hand, pantomimed a sawing motion in the air above the woman's wrist. "Give me a hand. Be easier to work with if I can take it back to the KPD lab with me."

"Ah" was the only syllable that came out of my startled mouth. This was a first for me, but Art was the expert, so—taking a scalpel from a tray of tools on the long counter, I cut through the tendons and ligaments of the left wrist, taking care not to nick any of the bones. I wrapped the severed hand in a paper towel and then zipped it into a plastic bag.

Art tucked it into the outside pocket of his jacket as casually as he might have deposited his car keys or a candy bar. "I'll let you know what I get," he said. "You about to start cooking?" I nodded. "Want me to help you get her into the pot?" I shook my head. "Darn," he said. "You never let me have any fun." With that and a wave, he was gone.

Ten minutes later so was I, leaving the corpse curled up in the kettle and the thermostat set at 150 degrees.

"**G**ag," squawked Kathleen when I dashed up the basement stairs and into the kitchen. "You *reek*." I headed toward her, my arms opened wide, as if to enfold her in a bear hug. "*Away*, vile one," she squealed, swatting at me with a dish towel. "Go back downstairs and take a long shower. Then take another one." I nodded obediently. "But first, go out to the garage and take off those clothes."

"Oh, baby," I said. "I do love it when you tell me to take off my clothes."

"In your dreams, stinky. Put them in the washing machine on *hot*." As I started down the stairs, I heard her calling after me, "The *old* machine. Don't you *dare* put those in the new one."

6

December 24

I CHECKED A THIRD time, and for the third time I came up one bone short. Actually, technically, I was forty-five bones short; the adult human skeleton contains 206 bones, and the skeleton I'd laid out on the counter had just 161. But the feet and ankles accounted for forty-four of the absent forty-five bones, so I'd already mentally subtracted those from the total. The unexpectedly missing bone—the maddeningly missing bone—was the one I'd been banking on to tell me how the woman was killed. "Where the hell's the hyoid?" I muttered.

As soon as I'd seen the woman's body in the woods, I suspected severe trauma to her neck—a slashed throat or, more likely, strangulation. When blowflies find a corpse, they seek moist orifices in which to lay their eggs: eyes, nose, mouth, ears, genitals, and, above all, bloody wounds. In this case, the soft tissues of the woman's neck had been completely consumed, exposing the cervical vertebrae. That told me her neck was particularly attractive to the flies—evidence that it had been bleeding or badly bruised. I'd seen no blood on the ground—and no knife marks on the vertebrae as I'd fished them from the steam kettle just now and laid them on the counter—so I felt fairly sure she'd been strangled rather than slashed. Trouble was, to confirm my hypothesis, I needed a hyoid—specifically, a hyoid crushed by a killer's lethal grip. And the hyoid was not to be found, no matter how carefully I sifted and squeezed the gooey residue remaining in the bottom of the kettle.

"Damned dogs," I muttered. The ends of the woman's legs were covered with gnaw marks, which indicated that her feet had been chewed off by canids—wild dogs or, more likely, coyotes roaming the hills of Morgan County. Had they also gnawed at the woman's neck? I studied the vertebrae again, this time looking for tooth marks rather than cut marks. There were none. Was it possible that some especially dexterous dog or coyote—seeking a particular delicacy—had managed to pluck the hyoid from the throat without doing damage to any of the adjacent bones? *No way*, I thought, then said again, "So where the hell is the hyoid?" Had I been so sloppy and careless, in my haste to get the corpse into the body bag, that I'd failed to notice a stray bone lying on the ground, right beside the exposed cervical vertebrae?

Frowning, I laid down the last of the vertebrae, shucked off my gloves, and opened the large envelope resting on the counter. I'd picked up the envelope at Thompson Photo on my way to campus. Inside, tucked snugly into slots in a sheet of clear plastic, were the thirty-six color slides I'd shot two days before, at the death scene in the mountains. As I'd spiraled in toward the corpse, I took half a dozen close-ups of the neck, including two from each side. Now, as I laid the slides on a light box and picked up a magnifying glass, I both hoped and feared what those close-ups might reveal: the woman's hyoid, and my carelessness.

In fact, the close-ups revealed nothing except what I remembered seeing: exposed cervical vertebrae, resting on a layer of dead, dry leaves. "Where the hell is the *hyoid*?" I was sounding like a broken record. I snapped off the light box, then, an instant later, I snapped it back on, realizing that something in one of the other slides seemed odd. It was the first photo I'd taken—the one with my zoom lens at its widest setting—and it was the last photo I'd have expected to reveal an important forensic detail. I stared at it, and as I realized what I was seeing, my understanding of the crime scene—and even the crime—was transformed.

In the upper corner of the photo, barely within the frame, was something I'd completely overlooked two days before: a dark, greasy-looking circle, a foot or so in diameter, located eight or ten feet up the slope from where the woman's body lay splayed against the tree. I heard myself say once more, "Damned dogs!" This time I said it with a laugh.

The body, I now realized, had not been posed by the killer in a shocking sexual display; the body hadn't been posed at all, in fact. The dark, circular stain marked the spot where the body had originally lain, the spot where it first began to decompose. The stain was a slick layer of volatile fatty acids, released as the body had begun to decay. The body's final resting place, against the tree—although perhaps "resting" was the wrong word—marked the spot where the dogs or coyotes had dragged it, en route to their den or some other sheltered spot, before the legs parted around the tree and the trunk stopped her downward slide. Picturing the scene in my mind, I imagined the confusion and frustration of the two coyotes on either side of the sapling as the corpse yanked to a halt; I imagined their disappointment as they were forced to settle for only the feet, their meager consolation prizes. "Poor doggies," I said, snatching up a small paper evidence bag and tucking it into my shirt pocket. Snapping off the light box again, I headed for the door of the Annex.

I stepped out into the cold, gray light of the late December morning, the sky swirling with low, ominous clouds. Then, on an impulse, I stepped back inside. As long as I was making the drive to Morgan County, I might as well get as much mileage from the trip as possible. No point showing up empty-handed.

7

Perimortem Revisited

THE COURTHOUSE CLOCK READ 9:05 as I got out of my truck and headed for the door of the sheriff's office. My wristwatch, on the other hand, read 11:45—the drive had taken an hour, and I'd made a thirty minute stop on my way into Wartburg. I smiled when I realized that the clock's hands hadn't moved since my prior visit. *Come to Morgan County,* I thought, composing an imaginary slogan for the Chamber of Commerce. *A place where time stands still.*

"He's not here," the sheriff's dispatcher told me.

"How about Deputy Cotterell?"

"Him neither. Nobody's here but me. They're all out with the posse."

"Posse?" Had the dispatcher actually said "posse"? "What posse?"

"They're after an escaped convict. They was out all night. A whole big bunch of 'em—a hunnerd volunteers, come from all over the place. Somebody called yesterday, sayin' they seen the guy down toward Coalfield. So the sheriff 'n' ever'body's down yonder." She looked me up and down, sizing me up, then asked, "Was you wantin' to join up with the posse?" Her tone was dubious; evidently I did not look like posse material.

"Heavens no," I said. "I've been looking at the bones of the dead woman—the woman whose body was found in the park on Friday. I've just found another bone out at the scene, and I need to show it to the sheriff."

She looked startled, then puzzled, then a glimmer of understanding dawned in her eyes. "Oh, you're that bone detective from UT," she said, and I nodded. "Was you needin' something? Anything I can do for you?"

I shook my head, but then I thought of something. "Actually, yes, maybe you can help me. Who's the best dentist in town?"

"Ha! That's easy. Ain't but one, anymore, now that Doc Peterson's passed on. Dr. Hartley. He's a lot smarter'n Doc Peterson was. Younger 'n' better lookin', too." She pointed. "Two blocks thataway, down Main Street. Big old house on the left. If the door's locked, try ringing the bell. He lives right upstairs."

Closed until January 2, read a hand-lettered sign in the leaded-glass door of Dr. Hartley's office, which occupied the ground floor of a two-story Victorian. Recrossing the wide front porch and descending the steps, I looked up at the second-story windows. The sky was surprisingly dark for midday; the swirling clouds seemed to be pressing down upon the house. Through wavy glass, I saw lights burning in two upstairs rooms, so I returned to the door and rang the bell. There was no response, and after a while I tried it again. Still no answer. *Third time's the charm,* I hoped, and pressed the button once more, holding it down long enough to show I meant business.

This time I heard rapid footsteps on a staircase, and then a light flicked on and an unhappy face appeared, fractured into odd angles and planes of anger by the beveled glass. A dead bolt snicked back and the door opened, the face unfractured now, but unhappy still. "The clinic's closed until next Wednesday." He tapped the sign for emphasis, and the panes rattled slightly within their channels of lead.

"I know," I said, "and I'm sorry to intrude, Dr. Hartley, but it's important. I'm investigating a murder, and I'm hoping you might be able to help me identify the victim."

The annoyance on his face gave way to a mixture of puzzlement and curiosity. "Are you with the sheriff's office?"

"No sir. My name's Bill Brockton; I'm a forensic anthropologist at the University of Tennessee. The sheriff brought me in to help ID the victim and determine the manner of death. I'm hoping you might recognize this dental work."

"Well, I'll be glad to help if I can. Do you have X rays of the teeth? Or dental charts?" His eyes narrowed as they took in the hatbox under my arm.

"Better than that," I said. "I've got the teeth themselves. The jaws, too. The whole skull, in fact. The dental work is quite distinctive."

His gaze shifted from my face to the box and back again. "Well," he said finally, his startled expression giving way gradually to one of mild amusement. "I must say, this is a first. Come in, have a seat, and let's have a look."

He sat behind a large wooden desk in an oak swivel chair, one that might have been as old as the house itself; I sat facing him in a high-backed wing chair, also an antique, the box on my lap. "I reckon I should ask if you're squeamish."

"Me? Lord no. Squeamish people don't make it through dental school—or didn't twenty years ago, when I was a student. Back then, they started us off dissecting cadavers. They don't do that anymore, but they should. Weeds out the weak, and teaches you the anatomy, inside and out. So no, a skull won't faze me in the least."

I nodded. "Just checking." I removed the box lid and set it on the floor, then lifted the skull from the nest of paper towels with which I'd cushioned it. I leaned forward, my elbows on the desk, and turned the face of the skull toward him, hoping for a flicker of recognition in his eyes.

Instead of a flicker, I saw a seismic shock. Hartley gasped, shoving his chair back from the desk so hard that his head hit the wall. He blanched, and a moment later he bent forward and scrabbled beneath his desk. I heard the clatter of a metal trashcan, and then I heard violent retching. It continued, off and on, for a minute or more, and when he finally sat up, the retching had given way to weeping.

"She said her horse had kicked her in the mouth," he whispered, "but I knew better. I knew that sonofabitch did it. A baseball bat, a two-by-four, a candlestick—I don't know what he hit her with, but whatever it was, it could've killed her." He shook his head angrily. "She always stuck to the script—she was too scared to tell the truth—but I knew. And she knew that I knew."

"Who is 'she,' Dr. Hartley? And who's the sonofabitch?"

"Denise Donnelly," he said. "The wife—the possession—of Patrick Donnelly." He said both names as if I should know them. He said the man's name as if I should loathe it.

"Sorry, I'm not from here," I said. "Who are they?"

"The richest people in Wartburg. Not that there's many of those. He's got mineral rights to half the county. Owns two or three strip mines—legal ones—and probably half a dozen wildcats." Seeing the puzzled expression on my face, he translated. "Wildcat mines are illegal, fly-by-night mines—no permits, no health and safety procedures, no environmental protection. Cheap, quick guerrilla raids on shallow seams of coal. Get in and get out, rape and pillage, before the regulators know you're there." He looked down, twisting a ring on his right hand, a haunted expression on his face. "I knew he'd kill her someday if she didn't get out. I begged her to leave him." Suddenly he shuddered and buried his face in his hands, and his body shook with the force of his sobs.

When he finally looked up at me again, the light in his eyes had gone out, and he seemed twenty years older than when he'd answered the door. And in that moment I understood. "I'm so sorry, Dr. Hartley," I said. "You're obviously shocked. And . . ." I wasn't sure if I should go on, but I did. "It's none of my business, but I gather that you and Mrs. Donnelly were . . . close, so I truly apologize for springing this on you." He nodded bleakly. "When did you hear she was missing?"

He blinked, startled. "I didn't. I don't think *anybody* did—a town this size, word gets around, you know? But I should have guessed." He looked away, and when he looked back at me, it was as if he'd decided something. "At first she was just a patient whose teeth I cleaned twice a year. Then, after . . . *this*"—he pointed at the skull—"she needed a lot of post-op care. I saw her every week for six months. And eventually . . ." He didn't need to finish the sentence. "She called me two weeks ago. Patrick had bugged the phone; he knew everything. She said she was going to California, to stay with her sister for a while, to sort things out. Told me not to try to contact her. Said it would just make things more painful for everyone." He drew a deep breath, and as he exhaled, his face seemed to harden. "Then Patrick took the phone from her. He said that if I ever called or spoke to her again, Denise and I would wish we'd never been born. Then he hung up. I hoped she'd find a way to call me again, but she didn't." He looked at the skull and gave a bitter semblance of a laugh. "Now I know why."

We sat in silence, the only sound the ticking of an antique clock. Then, in the distance, I heard the sound of car horns—faintly at first, then louder and louder, so numerous they blended together into one cacophonous clamor. A moment later a jubilant procession—or was it a riot on wheels?—roared past the dentist's house and up Main Street toward the courthouse.

"What on earth is that?" I said. And then—with a sudden, sickening feeling—I knew what it was.

I felt like a football running back, fighting my way through a hundred defensive linemen, as I forced my way through the whooping crowd surrounding the courthouse. Thunder rumbled overhead, as if the storm gathering on the ground were mirrored in the purple-black sky.

Two deputies, both armed with pump shotguns, stood on the steps and blocked the entrance. "I have to see the sheriff," I said.

"The sheriff's busy," said one.

"Interrogating a prisoner," smirked the other.

"That's why I need to see him," I said. "I'm with the state medical examiner's staff." I pulled my ID badge from my wallet and held it out, but the deputies seemed uninterested. "I know who the dead woman is," I went on. Now, for the first time, I had their attention. "I've just identified her."

"What's her name?" the first deputy asked.

"Take me to the sheriff," I insisted. "That information's for his ears only."

It was a spur-of-the-moment fib, but it was effective. The two deputies exchanged glances, and the first one— who seemed to outrank the second one—disappeared through the door. Several moments later the door opened and the deputy leaned out, beckoning me inside. He led me up to the third floor, into the jail, and down a row of cells. Deputy Jim Cotterell was standing at the end of the hall, just outside a cell door, his expression grim. As I approached, I heard a dull thud inside the cell, followed by a quick grunt and a slow groan.

"Sheriff? Here's the bone doc," said Cotterell. Peering through the bars into the cell's dim interior, I saw the sheriff step away from a hunched figure—a black man, bent nearly double, who slowly straightened. Blood trickled from his lips and nose and from a laceration on his right cheekbone. The man's left arm ended at the wrist—a broad, blunt stump— and his right wrist was encased in a filthy cast.

"I hear you got something to tell me." Sheriff Dixon stepped from the cell, his face glistening and his eyes glittering, and walked toward the far end of the cells.

"Two things, actually," I said. "The woman was named Denise Donnelly." His eyes flickered, but he didn't react as strongly as I'd suspected. "I gather she's a prominent citizen?"

"You might say that."

"But she hadn't been reported missing?"

"Not to me." His eyes bored into mine. "You sure it's her?"

"I am," I said.

"How sure? Ninety-five percent sure?"

"No. This time I'm a hundred percent sure. I showed her teeth—her skull—to her dentist." An expression I couldn't quite decipher flitted across the sheriff's face, and I wondered if the sheriff, too, knew about their affair. "She'd had extensive dental surgery—reconstructive surgery, to repair an injury. The dentist recognized the work instantly."

"Yates!" The sheriff's shout boomed across my ear. Down the hall, the deputy who'd brought me upstairs turned from the prisoner's cell and trotted toward us. "Pat Donnelly's outside," the sheriff told him. "Go get him. Tell him I need to see him." He looked at me again. "What else? You said you had two things to tell me."

"She was strangled," I said. "Her hyoid—a bone in the throat—was crushed." Reaching into my shirt pocket, I removed the evidence bag and carefully extricated the bone.

Three hours before, on my way into town, I'd stopped at the scene and, on hands and knees, sifted through the leaves on the hillside, at the stained spot a dozen feet above the body's final resting place. "Eureka," I'd proclaimed when I plucked the bone from the ground and saw the fractures: saw what had killed the woman.

But the sheriff gave the bone only a glance before turning away. I grabbed his sleeve, forcing him to look and listen. "Sheriff, I don't think the man you've got back there would be physically capable of strangling someone." I remembered a third thing—a phone call I'd gotten from Art Bohanan just before I left. Art hadn't yet found a match to the prints, but he did find something else interesting. "A forensic expert with the Knoxville Police Department took a set of prints from her left hand. She fought, Sheriff. She had skin under her fingernails. White skin. And one red whisker." He didn't respond, so I plowed ahead. "From what I hear, the Donnellys' marriage had some serious problems." For the first time, I seemed to have his full attention. "You might want to consider the possibility that Patrick Donnelly killed his wife."

I saw his jaw tighten. "I might want to *consider* the *possibility*?" His eyes narrowed and his chin lifted slightly. "I tell you what. *You* might want to *consider* the *possibility* of knowing where your job stops and my job starts. Now, is that ever'thing you had to tell me? 'Cause if it is, I've got an interrogation to get back to."

He turned to go. "Sheriff?" I said to his broad, sweaty back. He stopped and looked over his shoulder. "How'd she get there?" He held my gaze but didn't speak. "Where's her car?"

He shook his head. "No telling," he said. "Bottom of a quarry. Bottom of a river. In a chop shop, gettin' parted out. In a scrap yard gettin' shredded. I don't know, and it don't matter. But when I find out, I'll send you a memo. That make you happy?"

"You're saying this guy disposed of the car and then walked back into the mountains?"

"I'm saying it don't make a bit of damn difference where the car is," the sheriff spat. "The damn *car* didn't kill the damn woman, did it? This nigrah *pervert* killed the woman."

"I don't think so," I said. "I think she was killed somewhere else—maybe at her own house—and taken out there and dumped. That's why there was no car—no nothing—at the scene. Her body had been out on that hillside long enough to decompose. At least a week, I bet. Maybe two. Ask around, Sheriff—see if anybody saw her or talked to her in the past ten days. This guy escaped, what, forty-eight hours before she was found? The timing doesn't fit."

"Cotterell!" he roared. The deputy, who I felt sure had overheard our exchange, jogged heavily in our direction. "Get this man out of here and on his way back to Knoxville."

"Yessir." Cotterell took my elbow and steered me into the stairwell.

We were only halfway down the first flight of stairs when the sheriff bellowed the deputy's name again. "Get back up here," he shouted. "He's so fuckin' smart. Let him find his own damn way out."

Cotterell squeezed my elbow, then I felt him slip something into my hand. It was a business card embossed with the blue-and-gold logo of the Tennessee Bureau of Investigation, and below that, the words SPECIAL AGENT WELLINGTON H. MEFFERT II. "Get to a phone and call

Bubba, quick," he hissed. "They're fixin' to lynch this fella."

"Did you say 'lynch'?" I stared at him. "You can't be serious. This is 1990."

He shook his head. "Not in their minds it ain't. Dixon don't speak for everybody—he sure don't speak for me. But them people milling around? They're Klan. Outsiders, mostly—Carolina, Virginia, Alabama. Dixon called 'em in for his posse. His posse, their party. I'm tellin' you, this is a done deal. They're fixin' to string this man up right here, right now."

"Cotterell!" boomed the sheriff. "You get your fat ass up here!"

"Call Bubba," the deputy hissed, and hurried up the stairs.

Just as I reached the ground floor, the outside door opened and Deputy Number One—Yates?—entered. He was accompanied by a tall, barrel-chested man. He had red hair and a red beard. He also had red scratches on his face.

I ducked down a darkened hallway and found a vacant office. Switching on a desk lamp, I laid down the card and picked up the phone. It took several tries to get through—I had to push down one of the clear buttons on the base of the phone and then dial 9 for an outside line, and my trembling fingers misdialed twice. Finally, miraculously, I heard Meffert's voice.

My voice shaking, I recounted what I'd learned, what the sheriff had said and done, and what Cotterell predicted.

"Shit," said Meffert. "Shit shit *shit*."

"You really think they might lynch this man?"

"You remember what happened in Greensboro? Bunch of Klansmen shot up a crowd of black protesters. Killed six people, including a pediatrician and a nurse. That was in 1979. Two years later, in Mobile, they hung a black man from a tree, just to show they could. Sheriff Dixon's telling them a black sex offender has raped and murdered the most prominent white woman in Morgan County, Tennessee? Do I think it might happen? No—I *know* it'll happen. Take a miracle to stop it."

I was just putting the phone back in the cradle when I glimpsed movement in the darkness beyond me. An instant later a pistol entered my small circle of light. A hand aimed the pistol at my chest, and a voice—the sheriff's gravelly voice—said, "What do you think you're doing?"

"I was just calling my wife," I said. "I told her I'd be home by mid-afternoon. I didn't want her to worry."

"Now ain't that sweet," he said. "Let me call her, too, and tell her how much we 'preciate your help." With his free hand, he lifted the handset and pressed Redial. He angled the earpiece so that both of us could hear it ringing.

Don't answer, Bubba, I prayed.

"Meffert," I heard the TBI agent say, and my heart and my hopes sank.

"You get in there," the sheriff snarled, prodding me with the pistol, "and don't make me tell you twice."

Cotterell was in the corridor, a plastic cup in one hand, a blank look on his face. "Here, let me help you, Sheriff," he said, opening the cell door wider. "How about we cuff him, too? Here, hold my coffee for just one second?" Without waiting for an answer, the deputy handed Dixon the cup, then—to the astonishment of both me and the sheriff—he snapped one handcuff on his boss's outstretched wrist and, with a quick yank, clicked the other cuff to the cell door. As Dixon stared in bewilderment, Cotterell twisted the pistol from the sheriff's other hand and shoved him into the cell, the sheriff's movement pulling the door shut behind him.

"What the *fuck* are you doing?"

"I'm placing you under arrest, Sheriff."

"Bull-*shit*. What are you talking about?"

"I'm talking about assault. I'm talking about obstruction of justice. I'm talking about evidence-tampering, and conspiracy, and corruption, and probably civil-rights violations, too, though I reckon the D.A. or the U.S. Attorney will know more about that than I do."

"You're fired, Cotterell. And that's the least of your troubles. You unlock this cell and unlock these cuffs, and I mean *right* now, or I will *bury* you under this goddamn courthouse."

"I can't do that, Sheriff. I'm sworn to uphold the law, same as you. Difference is, I really aim to do it."

A cheer went up from the crowd when Cotterell and I emerged onto the courthouse steps, where one of the shotgun-wielding deputies still stood sentinel, but it quickly faded when the door closed behind us.

"Where is he?" shouted the big red-haired man I'd seen going inside earlier. *Donnelly*. "Where's that sick sumbitch that killed my wife?"

"Where is he?" echoed a jumble of other voices. "Bring him out!"

"Hang on, *hang* on," Cotterell called. "Y'all just hold your horses. Sheriff Dixon's still interrogatin' him."

"We already know ever'thing we need to know," shouted Donnelly.

"Yeah." I heard. "*Yeah!* Let's get it on!"

Suddenly there was a commotion to one side, and the crowd there parted, revealing a six-foot cross, its frame wrapped in layers of cloth—*wrapped in swaddling clothes*, I thought, in an absurd echo of the Christmas story—and a tongue of flame climbing up from its base and spreading to the outstretched arms. The crowd roared its approval.

"Come on!" yelled Donnelly. Someone thrust something into his hands, and I felt my stomach lurch when I recognized the distinctive shape of a rope noose.

Cotterell held up both hands in an attempt to quiet the crowd. "Not so fast," he yelled. "We might be gettin' ahead of ourselves. We ain't sure we got the right man."

"Hell *yeah* we got the right man," Donnelly jeered. "No doubt about it. Now shut up, Jim. Get with us or get outta the damn way."

To my surprise—to my deep dismay—I felt myself take a step forward. "Listen to me," I shouted. "You all are making a mistake."

"Who the hell are you," Donnelly bristled, "and what business is this of yours?"

"I'm a forensic scientist," I said. "I'm the one who identified your wife's body. The man inside didn't kill her." A wave of discontent rippled through the crowd. "Denise Donnelly was strangled. Her throat crushed. That man's a cripple—he couldn't have done it."

"He's full of shit," yelled Donnelly. "That nigger is a rapist and a killer, and he's got to hang." His words prompted a raw, enraged chorus of agreement.

"That man was behind bars in Brushy Mountain while she was being killed," I shouted. "She was already dead—long since dead—by the time he escaped." I fumbled at my shirt pocket, my shaky hand reaching for the small, folded paper bag—the bag containing the hyoid bone I'd plucked from the stained leaves on the hillside a few hours before. But before I could extract it, I was interrupted by a shout from the crowd.

"Nigger-lover," yelled someone deep in the pack, and the insult was taken up by dozens of voices. "Nigger-lover! Nigger-lover! Nigger-lover!"

Donnelly held up a hand for quiet, and the taunts died away. "We don't need some liberal, egghead *scientist*"—I saw spittle spray from his mouth when he spat out the word—"coming in here acting like he's better and smarter than we are. Go back to your library, professor, and stay the hell out of our business."

"I'm on the staff of the Tennessee State Medical Examiner," I said, reaching for my belt and grabbing my badge.

"I don't give a good goddamn about that," he shouted. "We got plenty of rope. It wouldn't take two minutes to cut another piece for you. And that oak limb is plenty strong enough for two men to swing from."

"Denise Donnelly fought for her life," I yelled to the crowd. "She had her killer's skin under her fingernails. A *white man's* skin, and a red hair, too." I pointed at Donnelly. "Y'all ought to be asking Mr. Donnelly here how he got those scratches on his hands and face."

Finally, my words seemed to be having some effect. The mob quieted, and I saw heads craning to peer at Donnelly.

"I got these scratches clearing a briar patch last week," Donnelly shouted. "Anybody wants to come see the brush pile tomorrow, you're more'n welcome. But anybody calls me a liar to my face, you've got a fight on your hands."

I played the last card I had to play. "She'd been unfaithful to him. He had a motive to kill her."

There were mutterings in the crowd—the sounds of doubt—and I felt a surge of hope. Suddenly, from high overhead, came the sharp sound of glass shattering, followed by a shout from a second story window of the courthouse. "Hey! *Hey!*" The heads of the mob swiveled upward. Deputy Yates leaned out the broken window. "It's the sheriff! They've got him handcuffed and locked in a cell up here!"

"The sheriff was breaking the law," shouted Cotterell. "Just like y'all are talking about doing. I couldn't let him do that. I can't let y'all do it, either."

"Get out of the way, Jim, before you get hurt," warned Donnelly. "Come on, let's get the sheriff out and give that nigger what he deserves."

The crowd surged forward. Cotterell snatched the shot-gun from the deputy beside him. He fired it into the air, and they hesitated, but only briefly, then surged again. He racked the slide and fired once more, but by this time the mob was already swarming up the steps. Half a dozen hands laid hold of my arms; another half dozen began pummeling my head and shoulders. Beside me, I sensed the same thing happening to Cotterell.

Suddenly my attackers hesitated, then froze, and over the shrieks of the mob, I heard the whine of sirens—many sirens, growing louder as they approached the court-house. Then I heard the squawk of a loudspeaker. "This is the FBI. Put up your weapons and disperse immediately, or you will be arrested. Put up your weapons and disperse immediately, or you will be arrested on federal charges."

The hands clutching my arms let go, the rain of blows ceased, and I felt myself sag against the door as I was released and my attackers began backing away. I heard a commotion—a din of voices shouting "FBI! Make way! Make way!"—and the crowd parted and fell back, their faces scowling and cringing, like dogs who've attacked in a pack then were routed and set fleeing, tails between their legs. A wedge of federal agents—a dozen or more, all wearing body armor emblazoned FBI, all carrying short-barreled shotguns that they looked ready, willing, and able to use—forced their way to the courthouse steps. A man in civilian clothes stepped from the crowd and huddled with one of the agents. He pointed at Donnelly and at three others in the front ranks, and four agents spun from the wedge and put the men facedown on the ground, cuffing them in the blink of an eye.

I heard angry mutterings and wondered if the mob might turn on the FBI agents, but over the mutterings there were more sirens and more commotion at the back of the square. Moments later a phalanx of uniformed Tennessee state troopers, led by Special Agent Meffert, mounted the courthouse steps and stood shoulder-to-shoulder facing the crowd.

Meffert conferred briefly with the ranking FBI agent, then from the top step called out, in a voice that might well have carried halfway to Knoxville, "You have two minutes to disperse. It is now 8:03. Anyone still on the courthouse grounds at 8:05 will be arrested. You'll be charged with engaging in a hate crime, and you will be cuffed and transported to arraignment in a United States criminal court. Make your choice, and make it fast. The man in that jail is not an innocent man, but he didn't kill that woman. Anybody wants to go to prison for trying to lynch him, step right up—your future beckons."

The crowd had fallen back, but it had not scattered. Meffert made a show of checking his watch. "Y'all got one minute," he called, then added, as if it were an afterthought, "Now, I don't know from personal experience, but I hear there's a lot of big black men in federal prison be glad to add a little white meat to their diet, if you catch my drift. Variety bein' the spice of life and all. Who wants to be first in line for that? Step right up, *step right up*, you cowardly sons of bitches. I'll drive you there myself. I'll even hand you the soap and point you toward the showers. Come on, by God!"

As his challenge hung in the air, the flaming cross flickered and went dark, the fire went out of the mob's eyes, and the men slunk away, by twos and threes and tens, their tails tucked between their legs.

When the square stood empty—except for the law enforcement officers and the cuffed men and the undercover agent who'd pointed out the ringleaders—Meffert turned to Cotterell and me. "Well *that* was fun," he said, shaking his head. "Jim, you interested in running for sheriff again? I'm thinking you might win this time around."

"I'll give it some thought," muttered Cotterell. "First, though, I got to go change my britches."

Meffert smiled, then clapped me on the shoulder. "Welcome to the Volunteer State, Doc. How you likin' it so far?"

I stared at him, then heard myself chuckle. Within moments the three of us were howling with laughter— laughter of relief and disbelief and, above all, gratitude for our unlikely deliverance—there on the courthouse steps.

Murder is as old as the human species, but the forensic work of the Body Farm is a modern weapon in the war on crime. Back in 1992, Dr. Bill Brockton—the promising young chairman of the Anthropology Department at the University of Tennessee—wages a baffling, deadly battle of wits with a sadistic serial killer, one who seems to be circling ever closer to Brockton himself. In the next Body Farm novel, Brockton finds his lifelong research mission . . . but risks losing everything he holds dear.

Enjoy a sneak preview of

CUT TO THE BONE

Available September 2013
From William Morrow
An Imprint of HarperCollins*Publishers*

Prologue

SOME WOUNDS HEAL QUICKLY, the scars vanishing or at least fading to thin white lines over the years. Some assaults are too grave, though; some things can never be set right, never be made whole or healthy again, no matter how many seasons pass.

In this regard, wounded mountains are like wounded beings. Cut them deeply—slice off their tops or carve open their flanks—and the disfigurement is beyond healing.

So it was with Frozen Head Mountain, in the foothills of the Cumberland Mountains of East Tennessee. In the early 1960s, Frozen Head's northern slope—thickly forested with hardwoods and hemlocks—was blasted and bulldozed away by wildcat strip miners to expose a thick vein of soft, sulfurous coal. Geologists called it the Big Mary vein, and for three years, Big Mary was illegally carved up, carted away, and fed into the insatiable maw of Bull Run Steam Plant, forty mountainous miles south. Then Big Mary's vein ran dry, and the miners and their machines—their dredges and draglines and stubby, hulking haul trucks—departed as abruptly as they'd appeared.

They left behind a mutilated mountainside, naked and exposed, its rocky bones battered by the sun and the rain, the heat and the cold. After every rain, a witch's brew of acids and heavy metals seeped from the ravaged slope, blighting the soil and streams in its path.

And yet; and yet. Nature is persistent and insistent. Years after the wildcatters moved on, kudzu vines began slithering into the shale, latching onto bits of windblown soil and leaves. Scrubby trees—black locust and Virginia pine—slowly followed, clawing tenuous toeholds in the rubble. A stunted sham of a forest returned, one instinctively shunned by birds and deer and even humans of right spirit.

And so it was the perfect place to conceal a body.

Like the mountain, the corpse was partially reclaimed by the persistence and insistence of Nature. A year passed, or perhaps two or three or five. One spring afternoon, a seedpod on a black locust tree split open, and half a dozen dark, papery seeds wafted away on a warm mountain breeze. Five of the six seeds drifted and sifted into deep crevices in the shale. The sixth spun and swirled and settled into a neat oval recess: the vacant eye orbit of a now-bare skull. By summer the seed had germinated, sending pale tendrils of root threading downward through fissures in bone and rock. One day a female paper wasp—a queen with no court yet—lighted on the skull, tiptoed inside, and began to build her small papery palace. And so was formed an odd ecosystem, an improbable peaceable kingdom: wasp colony, flowering tree, crumbling corpse.

The world contains a multitude of postmortem microcosms. Many remain forever undiscovered. But all leave some mark, some indelible stain, upon the world; upon the collective soul of mankind.

Some—a handful—give rise to reclamation or redemption.

PART I

And the earth was without form, and void;
and darkness was upon the face of the deep.

GENESIS 1:2

Now the serpent was more subtle than any beast
of the field which the Lord God had made.

GENESIS 3:1

PART I

Brockton

September 1992

TUGGING THE BATTERED STEEL door of the office tight against the frame—the only way to align the lock—I gave the key a quick, wiggling twist. Just as the dead bolt thunked into place, the phone on the other side of the door began to ring. Shaking my head, I removed the key and turned toward the stairwell. "It's Labor Day," I called over my shoulder, as if the caller could hear me. "It's a holiday. I'm not here."

But the phone nagged me, scolding and contradicting me, as if to say, *Oh, but you are.* I wavered, turning back toward the door, the key still in my hand. Just as I was about to give in, the phone fell silent. "Thank you," I said and turned away again. Before I had time to take even one step, the phone resumed ringing. Somebody else was laboring on Labor Day, and whoever it was, they were damned determined to reach me.

"All right, all *right*," I muttered, hurrying to unlock the bolt and fling open the door. "Hold your horses." Leaning across the mounds of mail, memos, and other bureaucratic detritus that had accumulated over the course of the summer, I snatched up the receiver. "Anthropology Department," I snapped. The phone cord snagged a stack of envelopes, setting off an avalanche, which I tried—and failed—to stop. I'd been without a secretary since May; a new one was scheduled to start soon, but meanwhile, I wasn't just the department's chairman; I was also its receptionist, mail sorter, and answering service, and I was lousy at all of those tasks. The envelopes hit the floor and fanned out beneath the desk. "Crap," I muttered, then, "Sorry. Hello? Anthropology Department."

"Good mornin', sir," drawled a country-boy voice that sounded familiar. "This is Sheriff Jim Cotterell, up in Morgan County." The voice *was* familiar; I'd worked with Cotterell on a murder case two years before, a few months after moving to Knoxville and the University of Tennessee. "I'm trying to reach Dr. Brockton."

"You've got him," I said, my annoyance evaporating. "How are you, Sheriff?"

"Oh, hey there, Doc. I'm hangin' in; hangin' in. Didn't know this was your direct line."

"We've got the phone system programmed," I deadpanned. "It puts VIP callers straight through to the boss. What can I do for you, Sheriff?"

"We got another live one for you, Doc. I mean, another dead one." He chuckled at the joke, one I'd heard a hundred times in a decade of forensic fieldwork. "Some fella was up on Frozen Head Mountain yesterday, fossil hunting—that's what he says, leastwise—and he found some bones at a ol' strip mine up there."

I felt a familiar surge of adrenaline—it happened every time a new forensic case came in—and I was glad I'd turned back to answer the phone. "Are the bones still where he found them?"

"Still there. I reckon he knew better'n to mess with 'em—that, or he didn't want to stink up his jeep. And you've got me and my deputies trained to leave things alone till you show up and do your thing."

"I wish my students paid me as much mind, Sheriff. Have you seen the bones? You sure they're human?"

"I ain't seen 'em myself. They're kindly hard to get to. But my chief deputy seen 'em yesterday evening. Him and Meffert—you remember Meffert? TBI agent?—both says it's human. Small, maybe a woman or a kid, but human for sure."

"Meffert? You mean Bubba Hardknot?" Just saying the man's name—his two names, rather—made me smile. The Tennessee Bureau of Investigation agent assigned to Morgan County had a mouthful of a name—Wellington Harrison Meffert II—that made him sound like a member of Parliament. His nickname, on the other hand—"Bubba Hardknot"—sounded like something from a hillbilly comic strip. The names spanned a wide spectrum, and Meffert himself seemed to, also: I'd found him to be intelligent and quick-witted, but affable and respectful among good old boys like Sheriff Cotterell. "Bubba's a good man," I said. "If he says it's human, I reckon it is."

"Me and Bubba, we figured there weren't no point calling you out last night," Cotterell drawled on. "Tough to find your way up that mountain in the damn daylight, let alone pitch dark. Besides, whoever it is, they ain't any deader today'n what they was last night."

"Good point, Sheriff." I smiled, tucking away his observation for my own possible future use. "Couldn't've said it better myself." I checked my watch. "It's eight fifteen now. How's about we—my assistant and I—meet you at the courthouse around nine forty-five?"

"Bubba and me'll be right here waitin', Doc. 'Preciate you."

Tyler Wainwright, my graduate student, was deep in thought—figuratively and subterraneanly deep—and didn't even glance up when I burst through the basement door and into the bone lab.

Most of the Anthropology Department's quarters—our classrooms, faculty offices, and graduate-student cubbyholes—were strung along one side of a long, curving hallway, which ran beneath the grandstands of Neyland Stadium, the University of Tennessee's massive temple to Southeastern Conference football. The osteology laboratory lay two flights below, deep beneath the stadium's lowest stands. The department's running joke was that if Anthropology was housed in the stadium's bowels, the bone lab was in the descending colon. The lab's left side—where a row of windows was tucked just above a retaining wall, offering a scenic view of steel girders and concrete footers—was occupied by rows of gray, government-surplus metal tables, their tops cluttered with trays of bones. A dozen gooseneck magnifying lamps peered down at the bones, their saucer-sized lenses encircled by halo-sized fluorescent tubes. The lab's cavelike right side was crammed with shelving units— row upon row of racks marching back into the sloping darkness, laden with thousands of cardboard boxes, containing nearly a million bones. The skeletons were those of Arikara Indians who had lived and died two centuries before; my students and I had rescued them from rising river reservoirs in the Great Plains. Now they resided here in this makeshift mausoleum, a postmortem Indian reservation beneath America's third-largest football stadium.

Tyler laid down the bone he'd been scrutinizing and picked up another, still not glancing up as the steel door slammed shut behind me. "Hey, Dr. B," he said as the reverberations died away. "Let me guess. We've got a case."

"How'd you know?" I asked.

"*A*," he said, "it's a holiday, which means nobody's here but me and you and a bunch of dead Indians. *B*, any time the door bangs open hard enough to make the stadium shake, it's because you're really pumped. *C*, you only get really pumped when UT scores a touchdown or somebody calls with a case. And *D*, there's no game today. *Ergo*, you're about to haul me out to a death scene."

"Impressive powers of deduction," I said. "I *knew* there was a reason I made you my graduate assistant."

"Really? You picked me for my powers of deduction?" He pushed back from the lab table, revealing a shallow tray containing dozens of pubic bones, each numbered in indelible black ink. "I thought you picked me because I work like a dog for next to nothing."

"See?" I said. "You just hit the deductive nail on the noggin again." I studied his face. "You don't sound all that excited. Something wrong?"

"Gee, let's see," he said. "My girlfriend's just moved four hundred miles away, to Memphis and to med school; I've blown off two Labor Day cookouts so I can finally make some progress on my thesis research; and now we're headed off to God knows where, to spend the day soaking up the sun and the stench, so I can spend tonight and tomorrow sweating over the steam kettle and scrubbing bones. What could possibly be wrong?"

"How long's Roxanne been gone?"

"A week," he said.

"And how long does medical school last?"

"Four years. Not counting internship and residency."

"Oh boy," I said. "I can tell you're gonna be a joy to be around."

The big clock atop the Morgan County courthouse read 9:05 when Tyler and I arrived in Wartburg and parked. "*Damn*, we made good time," I marveled. "Forty minutes? Usually takes an hour to get here from Knoxville."

Tyler glanced at his watch. "Sorry to burst your bubble, but it's actually nine thirty-seven. I'm guessing that's one of those clocks that's right twice a day."

"Come to think of it," I recalled, "seems like it was nine oh five two years ago, too, when I was here on another case."

The stuck clock seemed right at home atop the Morgan County Courthouse, a square, two-story brick structure built back in 1904, back when Wartburg still hoped for a prosperous future. The building's boxy lines were broken by four pyramid-topped towers—one at each corner— and by a graceful white belfry and cupola rising from the building's center. Each side of the cupola—north, south, east, and west—proudly displayed a six-foot dial where time stood still. I suspected that it wasn't just eternally 9:05 in Wartburg; I suspected that it was also, in many respects, still 1904 here. Sheriff James Cotterell, who stood leaning against the fender of the Ford Bronco parked behind the courthouse, would certainly have looked at home perched on a buckboard wagon, or marching in a Civil War regiment. Special Agent Meffert, on the other hand—one foot propped on the bumper—was a different matter. I could picture Meffert wearing a Civil War uniform, too, I realized, but Bubba's eyes somehow had a 1992 knowingness to them; a look that—Civil War uniform notwithstanding—would have branded Bubba as a modern-day reenactor, not a true time traveler.

I made the briefest and most perfunctory of introductions: "Sheriff Cotterell, Agent Meffert, this is my assistant, Tyler Wainwright"—and then Tyler and I transferred our field kit into the back of the sheriff's Bronco, a four-wheel-drive vehicle with enough ground clearance to pass unimpeded over a knee-high tree stump. The road to the strip mine was far too rough for my UT truck, Cotterell had assured me, and Meffert had agreed. Once we turned off the winding blacktop and into the pair of ruts leading up to the mine, I realized how right they'd been: I saw it with my jouncing eyes, and felt it in my rattling bones.

Cotterell and Meffert rode up front; Tyler and I sat in the back like prisoners, behind a wire-mesh screen, as the Bronco lurched up the mountain. "Last time I had a ride this rough," Tyler shouted over the whine of the transmission and the screech of clawing branches, "I was on the mechanical bull at Desperado's, three sheets to the wind. I hung on for twenty seconds, then went flying, ass over teakettle. Puked in midair—a comet with a tail of vomit."

"If you need to puke now, son," Cotterell hollered back, "give me a heads-up. You ain't got no window cranks nor door handles back there."

"I'm all right," Tyler assured him. "Only had two beers for breakfast today." He was probably joking, but given how morose he seemed over his girlfriend's move to Memphis, he might have been telling the truth.

Eventually the Bronco bucked to a stop beside a high, ragged wall of stone, and the four of us staggered out of the vehicle. The shattered surface beneath our feet might have been the surface of the moon, if not for the kudzu vines and scrubby trees. "Watch your step there, Doc," Cotterell warned over his shoulder as he and Meffert led us toward the looming wall. The warning was absurdly unnecessary—not because the footing was good, but because it was so spectacularly bad. The jagged shale debris left behind by the strip-mining ranged from brick-sized chunks to sofa-sized slabs.

"I'm glad y'all are leading the way," I told the backs of the lumbering lawmen.

"Be hard to find on your own," said the sheriff.

"True, but not what I meant," I replied. "I figure if anybody's going to get snakebit, it'll be the guy walking in front. Or maybe the second guy, if the snake's slow on the draw."

"Maybe," conceded Meffert. "Or maybe the two crazy fools sticking their hands down in the rocks, rooting for bones."

"Dang, Bubba," I said, wincing at the image he'd conjured. *"That'll* teach me to be a smart-ass."

"Man," muttered Tyler after a hundred slow yards. "Every step here is a broken ankle waiting to happen." The gear he was lugging—a big plastic bin containing two cameras, paper evidence bags, latex gloves, trowels and tweezers, clipboards and forms—couldn't have made it easy to see his footing or keep his balance. The trees were too sparse and scrubby to serve as props or handholds; about all they were good for was to obscure the footing and impede progress.

"Bubba," I huffed, "you came out with the guy that found the bones?"

"Yup," Meffert puffed. The TBI agent appeared to be carrying an extra twenty pounds or so around his middle.

"He said he was hunting fossils," I went on. "You believe him?"

"Seemed believable. Name's Ro-*chelle*. Some kind of engineer at the bomb factory in Oak Ridge. Environmental engineer. Maybe that's why he likes poking around old mines. Fossils plus acid runoff—a twofer for a guy like that, I guess. There's damn good fossils right around the bones. You'll see in just a minute." He paused to take a deeper breath and reach into a hip pocket. "Yeah, I believe him," he repeated, mopping his head and neck with a bandana. "He came into the sheriff's office and then brought us all the way back up here. No reason to do that, except to help, far as I can see. Hell, that shot his Sunday right there."

"You never know," I said. "Sometimes a killer will actually initiate contact with the police. Insert himself in the investigation."

"Return to the scene," grunted the sheriff.

"Sometimes more than that, even," I said. "An FBI profiler I worked with a few years back told me about a California killer who spent a lot of time hanging out in a cop bar, making friends, talking about cases. Ed Kemper—'Big Ed'—was the guy's name. When Big Ed finally confessed to a string of murders and dismemberments, his cop buddies thought he was joking."

Meffert shrugged. "This Rochelle guy seemed okay," he said. "He's got a high-level security clearance, for whatever that's worth. But like you say, you never know."

Fifty yards ahead, I saw yellow-and-black crime-scene tape draped around an oval of scrubby foliage and rugged shale. "Did somebody actually stay out here overnight to secure the scene?" I asked.

Cotterell made a guttural, grunting sound, which I gradually realized was a laugh. "*Secure* the *scene?* Secure it from *who*, Doc?"

Meffert was right about the fossils. Just outside the uneven perimeter of crime-scene tape lay a flagstone-sized slab of black shale, imprinted with a lacelike tracery of ancient leaves. Beside it, angling through the rubble, was a stone rod the length of a baseball bat. Its shape and symmetry made it stand out against the random raggedness of the other rocks, and I stooped for a closer look. Diamond-shaped dimples, thousands of them, dotted the entire surface of the shaft. "I'll be damned," I said to Tyler. "Look at that. A lepidodendron."

"A what?" Tyler set down the bin and squatted beside me. "Butterfly fossil?"

I nudged it with my toe, and it shifted slightly. "Close, but no cigar. Your Latin's rusty."

He laughed. "My Latin's nonexistent."

"Butterflies are Lepidoptera—'scaly wings.' This is a lepidodendron—'scaly tree'—a stalk from a giant tree fern. Ferns a hundred feet tall. Carboniferous period. That plant is three hundred million years old if it's a day."

Tyler grasped the exposed end of the fossil and gently tugged and twisted, extricating it in a succession of rasping clinks. He sighted along its length, studying the intricate geometry of the diamond-shaped pattern. "You sure this is a scaly stem? Not a scaly snake?"

"Those scales are leaf scars," I said. "Also called leaf

cushions. But they do look like reptile scales, for sure. Actually, circus sideshows used to exhibit these as fossilized snakes. You're a born huckster, Tyler." I stood up, scanning the ground ahead and catching a telltale flash of grayish white: weathered bone. "But enough with the paleo lesson. We've got work to do. Let's start with pictures." Tyler laid the fossil aside and opened the equipment bin.

A few years before—when I'd first started working with the police on murder cases—a detective at the Kansas Bureau of Investigation had taught me a crucial forensic lesson: You can never have too many crime-scene photos, because working a crime scene requires dismantling it; *destroying* it. The KBI agent's approach to crime-scene photography sounded like something straight from Bonnie and Clyde's bank-robbery playbook: "Shoot your way in, and shoot your way out"—start with wide shots, then get closer and closer, eventually reversing the process as you're finishing up and leaving the scene. Tyler had been quick to master the technique, and even before we stepped across the tape at the strip mine, he had the camera up and the shutter clicking. It wasn't unusual for Tyler or me—sometimes both of us—to come home with a hundred 35-millimeter slides from a death scene, ranging from curbside shots of a house to frame-filling close-ups of a .45-caliber exit wound.

As Tyler shot his way in, so did I, though I was shooting with my eyes and my brain rather than a camera. The pelvis: *female,* I could tell at a glance; *subadult; probably adolescent.* The size: *small—five feet, plus or minus.* As I zoomed in on the skull, I reached out to pluck a seedling that was growing beside it and obscuring my view. As I tugged, though, the skull shifted—bone grating against rock—and I froze. "I'll be damned," I said, for the second time in minutes. The seedling, I realized, wasn't growing *beside* the skull; it was growing *from* the skull—from the left eye orbit, in fact—something I'd never seen before. Wriggling my fingers gently beneath the skull, I cradled it, then lifted and twisted, tugging tendrils of root from the rocky crevices below. The seedling was a foot tall, the fronds of tiny oval leaves reminding me of a fern. As I held it up, with Tyler snapping photographs and the sheriff and TBI agent looking on, I felt as if I were displaying a bizarrely potted houseplant. "Bubba," I said, nodding toward the bin, "would you mind opening one of those evidence bags for me?" Meffert scrambled to comply, unfolding the paper bag and setting it on the most level patch of rubble he could find.

Leaning down, I set the skull inside the bag. "You gonna just leave that tree in it?" asked Meffert.

"For now," I said, bending the seedling so I could tuck it completely into the bag. "When we get back to UT, I'll take it over to a botanist—a guy I know in the Forestry Department—and get him to slice it open, count the growth rings. However many rings he finds, we'll know she's been here at least that many years."

"Huh," Meffert grunted, nodding. Suddenly he added, "*Watch* it!"

Just as he spoke, I felt a sharp pain on my wrist. I looked down in time to see a wasp pumping the last of its venom into the narrow band of skin between the top of my glove and the bottom of my sleeve. "Damn*ation*," I muttered, flattening the wasp with a hard slap. "Where the hell did *that* come from?"

"Yonder comes another one," Meffert said, "right out of the evidence bag." Sure enough, at that moment a second wasp emerged from the open bag and made a beeline for my wrist, drawn by the "danger" pheromones the first one had given off. Meffert's hand darted downward, and by the time I realized what he was doing, he had caught and crushed the wasp in midair, barehanded. "Sumbitches must be nesting in that skull," he said. I was dubious, but not for long; two more wasps emerged from the bag, both of them deftly dispatched by Meffert. We watched and waited, but the attack seemed to be over.

"You're quick, Bubba," I said, rubbing my wrist. "You that fast on the draw with a gun?"

He smiled. "Nobody's ever give me a reason to find out."

"Well, watch my back, if you don't mind."

I resumed my inspection of the postcranial skeleton, scanning the bones from neck to feet. "Y'all were right about the size," I said. "Just guessing, I'd say right around five feet. And female," I added, bending low over the flare of the hip bones. "And young."

"How young?" asked Cotterell.

I hedged. "Be easier to tell once we get the bones back to the lab and finish cleaning 'em up. But I'm guessing teenager."

"Any chance this is just some old Indian skeleton?" the sheriff asked hopefully. "Make our job a hell of a lot easier if she was."

"Sorry, Sheriff," I said. "She's definitely modern."

Meffert chuckled. "Isn't that what you said about that dead guy over near Nashville a couple years ago? The one turned out to be a Civil War soldier?"

"Well, she's lying on top of all this shale," I pointed out. "If she's not modern, this must be the world's oldest strip mine." I said it with a smile, but the smile was forced, and it was contradicted by the deep crimson my face had turned at the reminder of the Civil War soldier.

"Don't take it so hard, Doc," Meffert added. "You only missed it by a hunnerd-something years."

"Too bad that soldier didn't have a tree growing outta *his* head," the sheriff added. "Big ol' pecan tree, with a historical marker on it? You'da got it right for sure."

Meffert grinned. So did I, my teeth clenched behind drawn lips.

We rode in silence down the winding mountain blacktop road toward Wartburg. Tyler was absorbed in the fossil he'd brought back, his fingers tracing the intricate diamond patterning as if he were blind, examining it by touch alone.

For my part, I was brooding about the parting shots by the TBI agent and the sheriff. They'd been joking, good-naturedly, no doubt, but the conversation had stung, even worse than the wasp, and the sting took me back, in my mind, to the event they were dredging up. Just after my move to Knoxville, I'd been called to a rural county in Middle Tennessee, where a decomposing body had been found in a shallow grave behind a house. The remains were in fairly good shape, as rotting bodies go—pink tissue still clung to the bones—and I'd estimated that the man had died about a year before. In fact, we later learned, the dead man was Col. William Shy, a Civil War soldier killed in the Battle of Nashville in 1864.

In hindsight, there were logical reasons I'd missed the time-since-death mark so widely. Colonel Shy had been embalmed, and until modern-day grave robbers had looted the grave—looking for relics—the body had been sealed in an airtight cast-iron coffin, which had kept bugs and bacteria at bay. But those explanations sounded more like excuses than I liked. They also provided precious little comfort in court, I'd learned, again and again: Hostile defense attorneys in contemporary criminal cases took great delight in bringing up Colonel Shy, rubbing my nose in my blunder as a way of undermining my testimony against their clients.

Colonel Shy wasn't the only case where I'd been derailed by difficulty in determining time since death. Another murder case—a case I'd consulted on shortly before my move to Knoxville—still haunted me. A suspect in the case had been seen with the victim two weeks before the body had been found—the last known sighting of the victim—and the investigator and prosecutor pressed me hard: Could I testify, with certainty, that the murder had occurred then? "No," I'd been forced to admit, "not with any scientific confidence." As a result, the suspect had gone free.

Hoping to fill the gaps in my knowledge—determined to avoid such frustrations and humiliations in the future—I had combed through stacks of scientific journals, seeking data on decomposition. But apart from a few musty articles about insect carcasses—dead bugs found in bodies exhumed from old cemeteries—I'd found virtually nothing. Nothing recent, at any rate, though I had come across a fascinating handbook written by a death investigator in China centuries before, in 1247 AD—a research gap of more than seven centuries. The good news was, I wasn't the only forensic anthropologist who was flying by the seat of his pants when estimating time since death. The bad news was, *every* forensic anthropologist was flying by the seat of his pants.

The *interesting* news, I realized now, as Tyler and I reached the base of the mountain, and the road's hairpin curves gave way to a long, flat straightaway, was that the field was wide open. Time since death—understanding the processes and the timing of postmortem decomposition—was fertile ground for research.

The sun was low in the sky, a quarter moon high overhead, when Tyler and I passed through Wartburg's town square on our way back to Knoxville. As I glanced up at the courthouse belfry, still pondering ways to unlock the secrets of time since death, I found myself surrounded by markers and measures of time: A frozen clock. A fossilized town. An ancient fern. The bones of a girl who would never reach adulthood.

A girl for whom time had stopped sometime after wildcat miners had ravaged a mountainside; sometime before a papery seed had wafted from a tree and a wasp queen had begun building her papery palace in the dark.

Brockton

PEERING OUT THE GRIMY windows of my office on the second floor of Stadium Hall, gazing through the thicket of steel girders and concrete ramps, I glimpsed the emerald waters of the Tennessee River spooling past downtown Knoxville and the university. Most of the hundred-yard distance between the stadium and the river was covered in asphalt—parking lots and the four lanes of Neyland Drive—and the pavement shimmered in the late-summer afternoon, creating the illusion that the river itself might begin to boil at any moment. The Anthropology Annex, where I needed to go, was a small, freestanding building fifty sweltering yards away.

When I opened the door and stepped outside, exchanging the stadium's cool, dark corridors for the sun-soaked outdoors, I felt as if I'd entered a blast furnace. Behind me, bricks radiated the pent-up heat like an oven; ahead, the asphalt lay like a sea of lava, and as I swam across through the heat and humidity, my clothes grew wet with sweat, my shirt plastering itself to my back.

A half-dozen rusting air conditioners jutted from the corrugated metal walls of the Annex, their compressors chugging full blast—*full steam,* I caught myself thinking ironically as I tugged open the balky steel door and stepped inside. The air conditioners did manage to lower the humidity a few notches, but they hadn't made much headway against the heat, and none at all against the smell.

The Anthropology Department's main quarters—built by bricking in the wedge of space beneath Neyland Stadium's grandstands, decades before—weren't exactly prime real estate; far from it. But Stadium Hall was palatial compared with the Annex. In winter the Annex was an icebox, rattling in the wind; in summer, it was a solar oven, its metal panels creaking and popping in the heat. And no matter the season, it stank inside, for the Annex was where we did the dirty work of processing human remains: simmering and scrubbing; separating flesh from bone; removing life's lingering vestiges.

One corner of the processing room was taken up by an industrial-sized sink, which was flanked on one side by an immense steam-jacketed kettle—a cauldron big enough to simmer an entire skeleton—and on the other by a wide counter that ran the length of the wall. The counter was covered with blue surgical pads to absorb moisture from damp, freshly scrubbed bones, and when I entered, Tyler was laying out the last of the bones we'd brought back from the strip mine, neatly arranging them in anatomical order.

Normally I began my forensic examinations at the skull, but in this case—a case where the questions of age and sex seemed to converge, to entwine, in a pivotal way—I found my eyes drawn first to the pelvis, which confirmed what I'd thought in the field: female, beyond a doubt. The hip bones flared widely, giving them the distinctive shape that always reminded me of elephant ears; the sciatic notches—openings at the base of the sit bones where major nerves emerged from the lower spine—were broad, unlike the narrow notch of a male pelvis; and the pubic bone curved outward and down to create a concavity in her belly and birth canal, making room for babies that this particular female would never have.

But if her pelvis said "woman," her mouth whispered a different, sadder word to me: "child." If she had lived to be my age, the ripe old age of thirty-seven, her maxillary sutures—the seams in the roof of her mouth—would have begun smoothing out and filling in, eventually becoming nearly invisible. But the maxillary sutures in the skull I cradled upside down in my hand were rough and bumpy, the bones barely beginning to fuse. In fact, if I hadn't known from years of study that the bones were slowly joining, I might have concluded that something had struck the hard palate at its center, creating a cruciform pattern of cracks. But it was her life, not her palate, that had shattered.

Tyler studied my face as I studied the dead girl's skull. "How old you think she is?"

"Not old enough," I said. "Fourteen; fifteen, tops. But maybe only twelve or thirteen."

He frowned and shook his head—not in disagreement, but in dismay. "That's what I figured, too, but I was hoping you'd tell me I was wrong."

"Any skeletal trauma?"

"A couple healed fractures in the arms," he said. "One in the left humerus, the other in the right radius, about three inches above the wrist. But nothing perimortem. Nothing *I* could see, anyhow. Maybe you'll spot something I've missed."

I pored over every bone twice—with my eyes and with my fingertips—in search of a fresh, unhealed fracture, or the ragged nick of a knife blade, or a telltale smear of lead from a passing bullet—but there was nothing to be found. Finally, circling back to the skull once more, I shone a flashlight through the foramen magnum and peered inside the cranial vault, in case there was a fracture on the inner surface that might have ruptured one of the meningeal arteries, the arteries carrying blood to the brain. "I'm not seeing anything, either," I said. "Doesn't mean she wasn't killed. Just means that any injuries she had were soft-tissue trauma." I took a final look into the cranial vault. "Oh, hey, did you find a wasp nest in here?"

He reached up and plucked a small gray object from the narrow shelf above the counter, then dropped it into my palm. A dozen or so hollow, hexagonal cells made of dry, papery pulp, it weighed almost nothing. "It's a little crunched on the sides, from the forceps," he said. "Getting it out through the foramen magnum was like trying to pull a ship out of a bottle."

"Any more wasps on board?"

He shook his head. "Nah, I think ol' Bubba Ray Peckerwood done got 'em all."

"Careful," I cautioned. "If you slip up and call him Peckerwood to his face, Special Agent Meffert might just feel obliged to open up a can of whup-ass on you."

"Ha—let him try," said Tyler. "I'll lay some yoga on him. He'll never even know what hit him."

"What," I scoffed, "you're gonna meditate him into submission?" Tyler was a recent and enthusiastic convert to yoga, for reasons I didn't fully grasp. "Weren't you an athlete—a real athlete—once upon a time? Weight lifting or shot putting or some such? One of those manly sports dominated by hulking women from East Germany?"

"Hammer throw," he said. "The ultimate test of strength and coordination. But by the way, there *is* no East Germany. The wall came down three years ago, in '89, remember? 'Mr. Gorbachev, tear down this wall?' Ronald Reagan's finest moment. You're showing your age, Dr. B."

Summoning up my reediest old-man voice, I piped, "Back when I was a boy . . ."

"Yeah, yeah," he said. "Save it for the undergrads, Gramps."

Was he just kidding, or was there a slight edge in his voice? Worse, was there a kernel of truth in his jab? Was I fossilizing even before I turned forty?

Time was much on my mind these days. Time since

death was foremost in my thoughts. But time *before* death—my time; my sense of urgency about creating a research program to fill the gaps in my knowledge—that, too, was tugging at the sleeve of my mind.

"Hang on a second, Doc, I'm fixin' to put you on speaker-phone," drawled Sheriff Cotterell. I had swum back across the sweltering sea of asphalt to the stadium just in time to catch the call. "Bubba Hardknot's a-settin' right here with me, and I know he'll want to hear whatever you got to say."

I heard a click, then a hollow, echoing sound, as if the phone had been lowered down a well. "Hey, Doc," Meffert's voice boomed, from deep in the depths. "Whatcha got for us?"

"Not much, I'm afraid," I admitted. "I'll send you both a written report in the next couple days, but here's the bottom line. No skeletal trauma, so the bones can't tell us how she died. All they can tell us is a little about who she was. White female; stature between five foot one and five foot three; age thirteen to fifteen. I estimated the age by looking at the pelvis, the teeth, the epiphyses of the long bones and clavicles, the—"

"Excuse me, Doc," Meffert interrupted, "the *what*-ih-sees?"

"Epiphyses," I repeated. "The ends of the bones. In subadults—children and adolescents—the ends of the long bones haven't yet fused to the shafts; they're connected by cartilage, at what's called the growth plates.

That's how the arms and legs can grow so much when kids hit puberty. Toward the end of puberty, the epiphyses fuse, and the long bones don't get any longer; you don't get any taller. This girl's epiphyses weren't fully fused yet, so she hadn't quite finished growing. She had her second molars—her twelve-year molars—so she was probably at least that old. And her pelvic structure had started getting wider, so we know she'd entered puberty. But her hips were still getting wider, so she wasn't out of it yet."

"How can you tell *that*?" asked Cotterell.

"Good question, Sheriff. There's actually an epiphysis on the outer edge of each hip bone, too—it's called the iliac crest, and all through puberty, the iliac crest is connected to the ilium—the wide bone of the hip—by cartilage. It's another growth plate. Somewhere around age sixteen or eighteen, the iliac crest fuses. After that, the hips don't get any wider."

I heard a rumbling growl, which even over the speakerphone I recognized as Sheriff Cotterell's laugh. "Doc," he chuckled, "you ain't never seen my wife."

"Let me rephrase that," I said. "After that, the *bones* of the hips don't get any wider."

"What else you got?" said Meffert. "You hear back from your buddy in Forestry?"

"I did. That little black locust seedling was two years old. So she's been dead at least that long."

"And no more'n how long?" asked the sheriff.

"I don't know," I admitted. "Nothing in the bones to tell us. When did that wildcat mine shut down?"

"Twenty-two years ago," said Meffert, "in 1970."

"Then she died somewhere between two years ago and twenty-two years ago," I said.

"Twenty years? That's as close as we can nail it?" The frustration in the sheriff's voice was crystal clear, even though he was forty miles away.

"I'm afraid so, Sheriff. I wish I had more for you, but I don't. We need better tools and techniques for determining time since death."

"Got *that* right," he said. I was glad he and Meffert weren't there to see my face redden once more.

Satterfield

HE PICKED UP THE sheaf of pages and tamped their bottom edges on the kitchen table to align them, then turned the stack sideways and repeated the maneuver to even up the sides. Once the sheets were in perfect alignment, he inserted them into the three-hole punch and swung the lever down slowly. Closing his eyes to concentrate, he savored the slight variations in resistance as the steel posts punched through the five single-spaced pages, sheet by sheet by sheet.

A loose-leaf binder, already half filled, lay open on the table in front of Satterfield. Popping open the gleaming chrome rings, he threaded the freshly punched pages onto the stack, then clicked the rings shut and began rereading the text, twirling a pink Hi-Liter with the thumb, index finger, and middle finger of his left hand as he read. When he came to the description of the cut marks, he uncapped the marker and highlighted the passage: "The bones were severed with a curved tool of unknown type, the cutting edge having a curved shape approximated by the arc of a circle 3.5 inches in diameter."

A yellow legal pad and a mechanical pencil lay beside the binder. Setting down the marker, Satterfield picked up the pencil and drew a curved line on the pad, then—doubting the accuracy of the drawing—he pushed back from the table and went to one of the kitchen drawers. Rummaging in the drawer, he found a metal tape measure and extended the tape to 3.5 inches. Next he opened the cabinet containing glassware and held the tape across the mouths of various vessels until he found one—a coffee mug—whose diameter fit the description in the forensic report. Setting the mug on the legal pad, he ran the mechanical pencil one-third of the way around the base, then set the mug aside and inspected the neat arc he had traced. The shape puzzled him. Trying to imagine the head of an ax or a hatchet behind the curve he'd traced, he frowned; the arc was too steep to fit either of those tools. Besides, he suspected that both of those implements—certainly a hatchet—lacked the weight required to cut cleanly through bone in a single stroke. Rereading the highlighted passage, he concluded that he'd interpreted the text correctly and had drawn the curve accurately. That meant he simply needed to do more research. Tearing the perforated page from the yellow pad, he folded and tucked it into his pocket. Then, closing the binder, he returned it to its hiding place—the cold-air return of the ventilation ductwork—along with the box of stolen files, the mother lode of material he'd begun to build his plans around. Fitting the slotted grille neatly over the mouth of the duct, he flipped the latches to lock it into place.

He checked his watch. Home Depot would be closing in an hour, but Satterfield figured an hour was plenty of time. It wouldn't take him long to find just the right tool for the job, if Home Depot had it. Satterfield was a man who believed in having the right tool for the job, whether the job was cutting up a corpse or eviscerating an adversary.

Frowning, he hung the ax back on its pegs—the blade was too tall, the arc of the edge too shallow—and continued down the aisle. Next he picked up a maul, a wood-splitting tool whose wedge-shaped head was like a cross between an ax and a sledgehammer. The tool's heft was good, promising to strike with tremendous force, but again, the cutting edge lacked the curvature he was seeking. Satterfield took the sketch from his pocket and compared it with the edge of the maul. *Could I file it down?* he wondered. *Reshape it? Probably not,* he decided. *It'd take forever, even with a bench grinder.* He was mildly disappointed, but he was also intrigued; the puzzle—the quest—was challenging and invigorating, and solving it would be hugely satisfying: it would redouble his adversary's frustration, and underscore Satterfield's superior intellect.

"Help you, hon?" The question caught Satterfield by surprise. He looked over his shoulder at the questioner, a middle-aged woman in an orange Home Depot apron.

Stoop-shouldered and beaten-down looking, she fell somewhere on the spectrum between mousy and hard-bitten. She clearly had never been pretty, and now her face was drooping and folding in on itself, as if she were already losing teeth. He caught a whiff of stale cigarette smoke coming from her, which explained her leathery skin and ashen hue. Satterfield found her not merely unappealing but actively repellent, not that he was shopping for anything but a tool here anyhow.

"No thanks. Just looking." He turned back toward the display, folding the sketch and replacing it in his pocket, then drifted back toward the axes.

"Gotcha some trees need cuttin'?" she persisted. *Christ,* he thought, *is she working on commission? Trying for Employee of the Month?* "We got chain saws, too, next aisle over."

"No trees," he said flatly. He glanced over his shoulder again—she was still there—and then he slowly turned to face her. "No *trees,*" he repeated, cocking his head slightly, as if something about the word itself suddenly struck him. With a slight smile he added, "Just . . . *limbs.*"

"*Oh,* you're *prunin'.* How thick are the limbs?"

"Not very," he said. His eyes drifted from her face to her shoulder and then down her arm, and he reached out and took hold of her left wrist, encircling it completely with his thumb and middle finger. Startled, she yanked her arm, but he had a firm grip. She opened her mouth to protest—maybe even to yell—but he bore down hard, pressing his thumb into the bony side of her wrist, and all she could do was gasp now, her eyes darting in panic, the way the rabbit's had. "Not thick at all," he said, smiling, raising her arm for a closer look. "Probably about like this. Maybe not quite so skinny." He turned her forearm this way and that, examining it from various angles, still bearing down on the bone. Finally he let off, though her wrist remained firmly in his grip. "What do you recommend?"

She cleared her throat. "Well, if you're just cutting branches," she said, her voice strained and trembling, "a lopper might be what you want." She pointed her free hand toward the wall at the end of the aisle. Satterfield noticed that the hand was quaking; he liked that. He raised his eyes to study her face—her eyes downcast, her posture cringing, like a chained dog about to be beaten—and then he glanced in the direction she was pointing. When he saw the assortment of long-handled pruning tools there, he released her and walked wordlessly to the wall. The woman scuttled away, rubbing her wrist, keeping a wary watch over her shoulder.

Satterfield took one of the tools from the wall and spread the handles, causing the metal jaws to gape; then, as he squeezed the handles, the jaws clamped shut. The cutting blade looked powerful and wickedly sharp, but the edge was all wrong—straight as a ruler—and he frowned and hung the tool back on the wall. He was turning to go when he noticed that the there was more than one type of lopper. The one he'd inspected and rejected was an "anvil lopper," according to the shelf tag. Satterfield puzzled over the name for moment, then noticed that the cutting blade—the straight, sharp-edged blade that wouldn't serve his purpose—closed against a lower jaw that was broad and flat, like a small steel chopping block. *Like a little anvil,* he realized. Hanging beside the anvil lopper, though, was another lopper—with a different name, a different design, and a different cutting action. This one was a "bypass lopper," and it cut scissor fashion—the edges of the two blades sliding past one another as the handles were squeezed together. The blades weren't straight, like scissor blades, he noticed, with growing excitement. The tool's lower jaw was blunt edged and concave, to encircle and support a branch from beneath as the upper jaw—the sharp-edged, steeply curved, convex upper jaw—sliced into the limb from above.

The bypass lopper came in three sizes. The biggest had handles as long as Satterfield's arm; in addition, the jaws incorporated a cam to compound the handles' leverage, multiply their force. Satterfield took the tool down from its pegs and opened and closed the handles a few times. He nodded approvingly at the metallic friction he felt; at the precision and power with which the edges slid past one another.

A selection of rakes and hoes hung on the wall a few feet away, and Satterfield walked toward them, the lopper in one hand, swaying beside his right leg. The handles of the rakes were about an inch in diameter: about the thickness of his thumb, he noticed when he held up a hand to compare. Taking a step backward, he spread the handles of the lopper wide and fitted the jaws around the wooden shaft of a rake. He closed the handles slowly, feeling for resistance—just as he'd done earlier, with the hole punch—as the concave jaw hugged the wood and the sharp edge began to bite into the layers of grain. Once the edges were well seated, he gave a smooth squeeze. The rake's handle snapped with a dry pop, the amputated portion clattering to the floor as a razor-thin smile etched Satterfield's face.

He took a step to his right. The hoes had heavier-duty handles: hickory, by the look of it, and nearly twice as thick as the rake handles. Satterfield opened the handles wide and worked the jaws around one of the handles. The blade cut easily at first, but the going got tougher fast, the steel handles of the lopper bending under the strain as he bore down. Just as Satterfield feared the handles might buckle, the hoe's shaft snapped. It clattered on the concrete floor with a resonant, musical note, like the ring of a baseball bat colliding with a fastball. Satterfield bent and picked up the severed piece, studying the cross section closely. The cut was clean, but when he held the wood so that the ceiling lights raked across the cross section at a low angle, he could discern the cut marks, a myriad of ridges and valleys etched in the wood as the jaws had bitten through it. The marks were steeply curved, approximating the arc of a circle 3.5 inches in diameter.

Pocketing the piece of wood, Satterfield headed for the front of the store to check out. On the way home, he'd stop at Kroger, whose meat department sold big beef bones for soup, or for dogs. More tests were needed, but so far he had a good feeling about the bypass lopper.

He found a checkout lane with no line, and slid the tool across the stainless-steel counter. The young man working the register said, "Is that it for you today?"

"Only thing I need," said Satterfield, but then he added, "Whoa, wait, I take that back. One more thing." He backtracked two steps, to the end cap at the entrance to the checkout lane, and snagged a fat, striated roll of shrink-wrapped silver-gray tape. He stood it on edge and rolled it toward the scanner as if it were a thick slice from a bowling ball. With a broad smile and a worldly wink, Satterfield said, "A man can never have too much duct tape, can he, now?"

About the Author

JEFFERSON BASS is the writing team of Jon Jefferson and Dr. Bill Bass. Dr. Bass, a world-renowned forensic anthropologist, founded the University of Tennessee's Anthropology Research Facility—the Body Farm—a quarter century ago. He is the author or coauthor of more than two hundred scientific publications, as well as a critically acclaimed memoir about his career at the Body Farm, *Death's Acre*. Dr. Bass is also a dedicated teacher, honored as "National Professor of the Year" by the Council for Advancement and Support of Education. Jon Jefferson is a veteran journalist, writer, and documentary filmmaker. His writings have been published in the *New York Times*, *Newsweek*, *USA Today*, and *Popular Science,* and broadcast on National Public Radio. The coauthor of *Death's Acre*, he is also the writer and producer of two highly rated National Geographic documentaries about the Body Farm.

Like them on Facebook at www.facebook.com/JeffersonBassBooks.

Visit www.AuthorTracker.com for exclusive information on your favorite HarperCollins authors.